What Readers Are Saying about G.J.C. McKitrick and *A Walk in the Th*

"...McKitrick is a supe ... unique individuals r ... dialog is remarkably authentic, ... (particularly the heat) seem visceral...Th ... read."—*Luci Shaw, author of Adventure of Ascent: ... Notes from a Lifelong Journey; Winner of the Denise Levertov Award for Creative Writing.*

"...weaves together details to make an exotic locale vivid, while keeping the story moving briskly. Propelled by big themes of faith and life, *A Walk in the Thai Sun* never preaches, and avoids cheap sentiment, making for a satisfying read."—*Larry Matthews, writer & editor, Toronto, ON.*

"...deeply convincing... the gritty feel of truth... wrestles with...the deep human questions about right and wrong, faith and doubt, justice and evil..."—*Loren Wilkinson, Prof of Philosophy & Interdisciplinary Studies, Regent College, University of British Columbia.*

"A comparison with Graham Greene comes to mind—for the clarity of the prose, the exotic locale, the noir ambience, the dead-center dialogue, the complexity of characterization, and most of all for the subtle spiritual dimension of this writing...."—*Michael Mason, author of The Blue Umbrella and The Mystery of Marriage .*

A WALK IN THE THAI SUN

G.J.C. McKitrick

Moonshine Cove Publishing, LLC
Abbeville, South Carolina U.S.A.

This book is a work of fiction. Names, characters, places and incidents are products of the author's imagination or are used fictitiously. Any resemblance to actual events, locales or persons, living or dead, is entirely coincidental.

ISBN: 978-1-937327-46-0
Library of Congress Control Number: 2014941476

Book interior design by Moonshine Cove; cover design by Naomi Arielle, used with permission.

DEDICATION

To Annie for her infinite patience and support.

FORWARD

Michael Mason, Author of the bestsellers *The Mystery of Marriage* and *The Blue Umbrella*

All murder mysteries are essentially spiritual in nature, focusing on the quest for truth and justice. The protagonist sets out to discover and expose the facts of what happened and to bring wrong-doers to justice, and in this he acts as an accomplice of God. In most mystery tales the religious aspect of this mission is hidden, but in A Walk in the Thai Sun it spills onto the surface—like escaping blood—even as it is handled with utmost delicacy.

This novel is no ordinary murder mystery. It resembles that genre; in many ways it walks and talks like a murder mystery. But as the reader will soon discover, it does not fit that mold. To be sure, there's murder here, and mystery, and a cop/detective protagonist, along with plot momentum enough to keep the pages turning. However, all these elements are skewed in a way that makes for a more intensely personal work of art.

Take the page-turning. While the plot is certainly compelling, what pulls us even more is the setting, which is so minutely and masterfully observed as to constantly rivet the reader's attention.

Or consider the angle of mystery. In this book the big question is not the identity of the killer but how the living characters relate to the one killed. This is a story about the mystery of relationships: father and son, father and daughter, man and woman, friendships, cross-cultural relations, and ultimately the approach of humans to the divine, and vice versa.

At the climax of A Walk in the Thai Sun, a nexus of apparent coincidences prompts one character to reflect, "Kind of makes you want to believe in God, doesn't it?" to which another responds, "Sure, if your idea of God is a second-rate novelist."

Thankfully, the writer of these lines is no second-rater. A comparison with Graham Greene comes to mind—for the clarity of the prose, the exotic locale, the noir ambience, the dead-center dialogue, the complexity of characterization, and most of all for the subtle spiritual dimension of this writing, which is less a dimension than a pervasive atmosphere. The deepest mystery here concerns the one character who is both most consequential and most invisible. The identity of this hidden protagonist I leave to the reader to explore.

I first encountered this wonderful novel in serial form. I was in a writers' group with Greg McKitrick during the time he was composing it, and once a month, after a scrumptious dessert and some great conversation, we would listen, rapt, as the latest installment of the new work unfolded. I was enthralled then, and I remain enthralled after several readings. When Greg asked me to write a foreword, I thought I'd just quickly skim the novel to refresh my mind. But after one page I knew I was hooked again, and I treated myself to re-reading every word.

This is the mark of first-rate literature: that successive readings yield greater depth and increasing pleasure. I envy those who are about to embark on this journey for the first time.

ACKNOWLEDGEMENTS

At lot of folks were helpful in the writing of this book. During the initial writing stages I was in a critique group with Michael Mason, Ron Reed, Tim Anderson and Karen Cooper. Constructive criticism and encouragement from those four friends played the largest part in getting this book written. After the initial draft was completed, editors Nicola Aimé and Kevin Quast helped to shape it into its current form. Also involved were beta readers Karen Probert, Joanne Bell, Alicia Merlyn, Bruce Ehlert, Lea Kulmatychi and Deborah Fieguth. Ken and David Fast helped produce the trailer. Naomi Arielle's painting graces the front cover. My mother, Ruth McKitrick, has always been supportive, as have my sons Sam and Isaac, and my brother Roy and his wife Debbie. Encouragement and various helps were also given by Barb Galler-Smith, Susan MacGregor, Ann Marston, Linda Pedley, Dal Schindell, Loren Wilkinson, Brian Buss, Stuart Appenheimer, Joan Dosso, Keith Johnston, Dennis Cahill, Chris Wiseman, Molly Shire, Ian and Maybeth Roberts, Tim and Brenda Noble, Rien and Maaike De Bell, Ken and Mary Widmer, John and Virginia Casto, Tom and Bonny Major, the Scruffies, The Strathcona County Writers Federation, and the Edmonton Writer's Group. Finally John Martin McKitrick, my father, who passed away around the time I started writing this and was always supportive of my creative endeavors.

PREFACE

My wife, Annie, and I lived in rural Thailand between 1986 and 1990 and I drew on experiences we had during that time to write this book. This novel is set in the late 1980s for that reason.

A WALK IN THE THAI SUN

CHAPTER ONE

Sam Watson peeled the tops back from two plastic cream containers and poured the contents of both into his coffee. This he stirred and then took out a cigarette and lit it. He took two long pulls and then gave his attention back to Jeff. His son was busy adjusting his carry-on bag. Jeff's wheat blond hair was longish and parted down the middle, the two front ends curving inward like pincers whenever he leaned forward.

"You sure you don't want something?" Sam asked.

Jeff looked up. "They'll serve us within an hour of lift-off and it's included in the airfare. I'll be fine until then."

"You're too disciplined for your own good."

Jeff smiled. "On our support level, you have to be."

"Your father is willing to buy you a coffee and a piece of pie, you know, even at airport prices."

"I know, Dad. But really I'd rather not, Okay?"

"I'll bet you didn't even spend any of the money I've sent you last Christmas."

Jeff said nothing.

"Well, did you?"

"I spent it."

"On what?"

Jeff studied his father for a moment before answering. "Cassettes."

"Cassettes?"

"Yes."

"Didn't you tell me you could buy good copies of pop albums for about a buck apiece in the markets over there?"

"Well, yes."

"Now let's see...I sent you three hundred dollars. That means you bought three hundred cassettes?"

"Six, actually."

Sam drank from his coffee, flicked the excess ash off his cigarette, and sighed. "That money was for you, Jeff."

Jeff gave his father a weak smile and said nothing.

"There are a lot of Asians here, you know. At least half a million...maybe even a million. It's not like you have to go ..."

Jeff held up his hand. "I have a call, Dad, a call to work among the people of Thailand in Thailand. I have to go. Otherwise they'd all have to come here to hear the Gospel. Which is easier?"

"The call, ah yes 'the call'..." Sam shook his head slowly. Why was it that his own son was the only person on the planet that made him feel completely helpless? "I'm sorry, Jeff."

"I'll miss you too, Dad."

* * *

Ute went out from the police box into the Thai sun. He could almost feel his skin turning brown as he stood looking down the road. Brown skin was peasant skin, the skin of those who did their labors in the sun, the skin of those who had no future. He put on his hat. Ute was fair, with a wave to his thick black hair and a slight crook in his smile. It made his way with women easy, a bit of good karma.

A 90cc Honda motorcycle with a yellow-helmeted driver approached from the north. He instantly recognized the combination, the young Christian missionary from Canada. He probably owned the only yellow motorcycle helmet in the entire province. He gave Ute a cheery wave as he passed by, on his way, no doubt, to the tiny Christian church in Khoksamrong. Ute had never been there but he had heard the church was full of lepers.

There was nothing else of interest on the road, only a *songtaow* that had stopped by a large mango tree to let off a passenger and her baskets of vegetables. The vehicle, a grey one-ton truck with two benches in the back and a canvas roof, was one of many that drove down the road at ten-to-fifteen minute intervals picking up anyone who happened to be waiting. For five *baht* one could ride to Banmi, the next market town.

Practically everyone in this *songtaow*, a group of perhaps twenty, had disembarked to allow the woman's four baskets of vegetables to be unloaded. She paid the driver and then turned to arrange her baskets in the shade by the side of the road. She sat beside them, put a plug of betel nut in her mouth, and began chewing, waiting for the next pedicab driver to happen by and take her, and her vegetables, to the village.

Ute looked back through the door into the police box. Kwanchai, his partner, was asleep on the bench. Ute sighed. Barring some major crime, the two of them would be off in an hour. It hadn't been much of a day, half a dozen traffic citations and a couple of one-hundred-*baht* “gifts” from logging trucks bearing illegal timber. He had been doing traffic detail for nearly three months, his reward for challenging the “official version” of what happened when he foiled a gem shop robbery in Banmi a few months earlier. That version had given the credit to Lieutenant Lup Law, his superior, who wasn't even in town at the time.

Ute looked down the road toward the woman and her baskets again. There was a small lime-green pickup with a canopy bearing down on her from the opposite direction. It seemed to be heading right for her, but at this distance it was probably heat distortion rising from the road. He turned away. A sudden distant screech brought his eyes back to the truck. One of the baskets, now empty of its vegetables was rolling in a spiral towards the middle of the road. The woman was on her feet swearing at the driver of the pickup. The driver and a passenger got out of the truck to survey the damage. Ute climbed on his motorcycle.

The passenger shouted at the driver and pointed in Ute's direction. The driver saw Ute and bolted into the trees. The passenger glanced back quickly at the truck, hesitated, and then followed the driver. Ute pulled the motorcycle up beside the woman and shouted for them to stop. Neither man paid any attention and they were soon out of sight.

Ute watched them disappear. It seemed absurd to flee the scene of an accident when the only damage was a spilled basket of vegetables. He looked at the truck idling in the midst of squashes, cucumbers, and tomatoes.

"Did you see what he did?!" the woman yelled. "Did you see?"

"Yes, ma'am, I saw," Ute said, still studying the truck.

"Well, aren't you going to chase them?" she asked, practically pushing her face into his. Years of chewing the mildly-narcotic betel nut had reddened her gums, teeth, and lips to the point that her mouth looked like an open sore.

Ute turned away, walked behind the truck, and opened the patched-canvas canopy. In the back of the truck, pressed up against the cab, were three full burlap bags.

"I said, 'Aren't you going to chase them?' " the woman persisted.

"No, ma'am, I'm not."

"Why not? They almost killed me and look what they did to my vegetables!"

"No backup," said Ute. He crawled into the back of the truck and took out his pocketknife. The bags, he discovered, had two layers, the outer burlap and an inner layer of thick plastic. An incision yielded a white powder. He took a small amount of the powder, rubbed it between his thumb and fore finger until most of it had fallen away, and then tasted it. A smile spread slowly across his face.

When he backed out of the pickup, he found the woman busy salvaging what she could of her vegetables. She did not even look at him as he mounted his motorcycle and started it up. Evidently she had decided that she would get no satisfaction from him. This suited Ute just fine.

"Kwanchai, Kwanchai! Come on wake up! There's something I want to show you!"

Kwanchai slowly sat up on the bench, shielded his eyes, and tried to focus on Ute's backlit form in the doorway. Kwanchai had stocky build, a cheap brush cut, and a thin red mark across his face where it had been in contact with the hard edge of the bench. He began rubbing this. "What's the matter?" he mumbled.

"I had a little fun while you were asleep. Come and take a look." Ute turned and began walking toward the pickup. Kwanchai followed him out into the sun. Beside the pickup, a pedicab driver was now helping the old woman load the baskets of vegetables on to his three-wheeled bike. Even from this distance Ute could hear the woman's loud monologue about how useless the police were.

"What's her problem?" Kwanchai said, catching up.

"The driver of the pickup lost control of his truck and knocked over one of her baskets. I saw the whole thing happen and, as I was riding toward them, the driver and his passenger ran into the woods. Wait until you see what I found in the back of the truck."

The old woman glared at them as she mounted the pedicab. Ute ignored her but Kwanchai gave her an apologetic smile.

"Take a look at this," Ute said, climbing into the pickup.

"What is it?" Kwanchai asked, peering at the burlap bags in the back of the truck.

"My ticket out of that box," he said gesturing back down the road. He collected a little of the powder and put it in Kwanchai's palm.

Kwanchai sniffed at the powder. His eyes widened, "How much is there?"

"At least a hundred kilos." Ute leaned back against the pickup and grinned.

"Don't you think we'd better get after them?" Kwanchai asked.

"On foot through that?" Ute gestured at the thick woods by the side of the road.

"Well..."

"Remember it's two on two and these guys were transporting heroin. They know the law as well as you do. Do you think they're going to put much value on our lives under the circumstances?"

Kwanchai frowned. "We'd better call in for reinforcements."

Ute shook his head. "No. At least not yet. I want to make sure lots of people know who found this stuff before it gets back to Lup Law. Otherwise he'll take credit for the whole thing. Besides, it'll take us at least half an hour to get backup out here. Those guys will be in Laos before then."

Kwanchai looked doubtful and then nodded agreement. "So what do you want to do?"

Ute studied Kwanchai for a moment before answering. His partner had been a cop for seven years longer than he had. He was supposed to be the senior partner, to be in command. Ute smiled to himself. "Well, we'll have to get this truck back to the station, of course. Why don't you do that? The key's in the ignition. Tell them we'll file a report on it later and don't let on what's in the back. Then meet me over at Charlie's."

Kwanchai considered this and then nodded slowly in agreement.

* * *

Lieutenant Lup Law made one last attempt to give his attention to the pile of papers in front of him and then took out a cigarette and lit it. He placed it into the right side of his mouth directly below two nearly parallel scars on his lower cheek, souvenirs from a dog attack when he was a small child. He puffed on the cigarette for a few moments, and then looked at the papers again. He fingered the new amulet around his neck. It was supposed to bring him luck.

"Lieutenant, sir?"

Lup Law released the amulet and looked over at Kwanchai standing in the doorway. The officer bowed to him in a self deprecating way.

"What can I do for you, Kwanchai?" Lup Law said.

"I have something I think you'd better come and take a look at, Sir."

"Really? What's that?"

Kwanchai's eyes seemed to search the wall for hidden menace. "I-I-I think you'd better just come and look, Sir."

Lup Law studied Kwanchai. "All right. Where are we going?"

"Just down to the parking lot, Sir."

"The parking lot?"

"Yes, Sir."

Lup Law gestured for Kwanchai to lead the way and then followed the younger officer down the back stairs.

* * *

"...and when they saw me coming toward them on the motorcycle, they just ran into the woods," Ute laughed. It was a long loud laugh fueled by too much drink. He had just spent two hours at Charlie's telling and retelling the story. "So I thought to myself, why are they running from me when all they've done is knock over a basket of vegetables? The worst thing that could happen is that they get a reprimand and a small fine. Hardly worth abandoning a truck for. So instead of giving chase, I decided to see what was in the truck."

He shook his head. "There's got to be a hundred kilos of heroin in there, Sir."

"And where is it now?" Lup Law asked.

"It's still in the truck, and that's parked outside."

"You just left a hundred kilos of heroin in a truck?"

"Well, Sir... It's only been there for a few minutes. And I didn't want to disturb anything in case you wanted to check for prints and things like that."

Lup Law stood up. "Come on, then. Let's go take a look."

It was now late afternoon and the midday heat was just beginning to dissipate. A few police officers had gathered under a shelter next to the station to smoke cigarettes and socialize. They watched Ute as he led the lieutenant across the parking lot.

"Is this it?" the lieutenant asked as he approached the truck.

"Yes. The stuff's in three bags in the back."

Lup Law gave Ute a long sideways look before opening the back of the truck. He then opened the canopy and crawled in without hesitation. Ute looked across the parking lot at the men under the shelter. One of them gave him a little wave.

"Are you sure this is the right truck?" the lieutenant said from inside the canopy.

"Yes. Why?"

The lieutenant crawled out of the back of the truck and began dusting off his knees. "The bags are full of cement." He started walking back to the station.

* * *

Sam Watson felt for the keys in his coat pocket. Their edges were sharp, irritating his hands. The locksmith made them yesterday. It was the third time he'd lost his keys in less than a year. He wondered why he found it so easy, these days, to think about such trivial things while working.

The photographer was busy snapping the girl's body from a variety of angles. Sam could see her nose had been broken long enough before her death to allow some swelling to occur. Dried blood flaked from her lips and chin, and the angle of her left thumb told Sam it was dislocated or perhaps broken. Long greasy black hair, matted with blood from the top of her head, partially hid puncture marks on both arms. She was fourteen, maybe fifteen. He studied the face again—familiar somehow, but he couldn't place it.

Sam looked around for a weapon but there was nothing obvious. He shuffled his feet and felt one kick something, a cardboard box from a donut shop. It was one of several such containers littering the floor around the old mattress where they had found the girl. The only other piece of furniture was a wooden chair freshly painted bright yellow. On this were a few pieces of clothing and an old Radio Shack ghetto blaster. Sam popped this open and pulled out a cassette. This too was Radio Shack, with the words "Cowboy Junkies" handwritten on the label. He replaced it, closed the machine and looked around the room again.

Only new paint in the place was on the chair. The pale yellow walls were mottled with mold and the window was cracked. The main doorframe was bent and the area around the lock showed evidence of numerous past attempts at prying the door open. These days a good shove was all it took. Like many of the rooms in the hotels of Vancouver's eastside, what was inside would normally need little security. This was the subsistence zone. You had to be pretty desperate to steal anything found here, but then again desperation was the defining characteristic of the area.

"Do you know her?" asked a voice behind him.

Sam glanced over his shoulder at Collins, who had just entered the room. Collins was nearly twenty-five years Sam's junior, a college cop recently promoted to lieutenant. "No." Sam lit a cigarette. "This was all we found when we got here. One of the other residents called and complained about a lot of screaming, banging, and crashing in the next room. We found the door to the room wide open and her lying there dressed only in a T-shirt. Paraphernalia all over the place. Tony is next door talking to the guy who called."

The two men stood aside as the paramedics placed the body on a stretcher and covered it. Sam and Collins watched silently as they carried her past and into the hall.

"Just think, Watson, only three more months of this stuff."

"Just think, Collins, you've got another twenty-five years of it, if you make it."

"I'll make it."

Sam studied Collins. The lieutenant was in his early thirties, but he'd been with the force nearly eight years. He was thoroughly cop, both in his attitude and social life. "Yeah, you probably will," Sam said. He stepped into the hall and took one last look at the girl. As he did, the covering slipped off her face. Then he knew.

"What's wrong?" Collins asked. "You look like you've just seen a ghost."

"The daughter of a ghost," Sam said almost in a whisper.

"What?"

Sam nodded toward the receding stretcher. "Her name was Nicki. She was the daughter of a hooker I used to know back when they were all working Davies Street. Nicki was only four or five the last time I saw her. I guess that's why I didn't recognize her right away."

"The daughter of a hooker?"

"Yeah, a hooker. Same one they found in the dumpster down on Homer a year ago last June."

"Well, at least they got the guy."

"Didn't help Nicki, did it?"

Collins said nothing.

In the silence Sam took his keys out of his pocket and looked at them. The keys worked, even though they looked nothing like the originals.

"New keys," said Collins matter-of-factly.

"Oh, you're good," Sam stuffed the keys back into his pocket.

* * *

Ute was no longer a person. He gave up his personhood when he entered the monastery six months earlier. He was now a *phra*, a monk, counted with the Buddha statues, the amulets, and other sacred things of Buddhism. He was a sacred object, a holy "it."

He walked down the street, eighth in a line of twelve monks, carrying food bowls in the early morning. As a Buddhist monk, he had a right walk down the streets and alleys at dawn receiving offerings of rice, fruit, and vegetables. A woman put a spoonful of rice in his bowl. He did not thank her or even look at her. He fulfilled a function, acting as the means by which the woman earned good karma. They both understood that.

Ute tried to keep his eyes on the monk in front of him. He tried to be dispassionate, unaffected by what went on around him. When the people looked at him, they were supposed to see a spiritual being walking along the road to enlightenment, but whenever his eyes strayed and he saw his reflection on the glass of the storefront windows, he winced.

The line of monks slowly began making its way back to the monastery as the sun climbed higher in the sky. At the abbey they would eat the food given to them, receive spiritual instruction, meditate, work on temple grounds, and care for stray dogs.

Ute walked slowly back to his quarters. He had eaten and he had listened to the Abbot talk about the impermanence of all things, about suffering and how it was the result of attachment to the transient things in one's life. Now it was time to begin the meditations, to begin the various exercises that were designed to release him from his attachments. It was the part of day he dreaded most. He could not attend to the sound of his own breathing, mull over the teachings of the Abbot, or in any other way quiet his mind. The best he could do was put on a mask of serenity to fool the others.

When he assumed various meditation postures and began the exercises, peace did not come, not a sense of calm, and no detachment from the impermanent things in his life. What came was yet another replay of his loss of face before his fellow police officers, and the laughter. What came was Lup Law's latter amazing discovery of a single thirty-five kilo bag of pure heroin in a squatter's shack down by the railroad, his subsequent appointment to the captaincy, and a new BMW that did not come with the job.

What came to Ute was hatred and a desire for revenge.

Ute could not satisfy this desire. Everyone he knew feared Lup Law and, by himself, Ute could do nothing. So he strove to defeat the desire itself, to control it, to rise above it. For an hour and a half he grappled with it, trying to trick his mind into going elsewhere. He tried to empty his mind of thought, grasped at every image of serenity he could think of, and finally forced himself to breathe so deeply that he nearly passed out.

Ute stepped out into the bright sun and squinted. When his eyes adjusted, he noticed Bom. The sixteen-year-old novice sat under a bo tree meditatively puffing on a cigarette, his legs arranged in proper lotus style. Bom had been left in the care of the monks when he was only seven years old and had grown up at the temple. He clung to Ute, hoping the former police officer would use his connections to find him a job so he could leave the place.

"Where are you going today?" Bom asked.

Ute did not answer immediately. He had several rotating destinations for his daily penitential walking meditations. "To the high school," Ute said finally, knowing that Bom would want to come along no matter what he said.

Bom stood up. "Good place. Good place. I like to Xray the girls as they come out of their classes."

"I'll be walking without sandals and avoiding the shade."

"A little pain and discomfort to blot out the past?"

Ute said nothing and began walking through the hot dust toward the temple gate, all the while attending to the precise movements and sensations of his feet. Bom grinned, slipped on his sandals, opened his umbrella, and followed.

"You know the first thing I'm going to buy when I get out of that place?" Bom asked, breaking a silence that had lasted nearly half an hour.

"No, what?" Ute said. His attempt at walking meditation was going poorly.

"One of those new Honda water-cooled Scramblers!" Bom's eyes seemed to glaze over. "You can really sit high in the saddle on one of those things. You could hit a buffalo and go right over it without feeling a thing. A truly amazing bike!"

Ute smiled. "They're nearly 45,000 *baht*, you know."

Bom dismissed the cost with a wave of his hand. "I'll get the money somehow, even if I have to go into debt for the rest of my life."

"You probably will," Ute said as they neared the school.

There was a small restaurant across from the school gates. They sat in the cool under the awning and ordered two Pepsis. As monks they were not allowed to eat solid food after midday but liquids were permitted. The woman poured two iced bottles of Pepsi into plastic cups, handed them to the two monks, and bowed before them. Ute and Bom ignored her. They were again being used by someone to earn good karma.

The students began to trickle out of their classes and make their way home. The young men wore black shorts and white shirts. Their names and the name of the school were sewn in blue across their shirt pockets. Black socks in various stages of disintegration clung to their ankles and descended into brown canvas shoes. Their hair was cut short in the manner of new military recruits.

The young women also wore uniforms, black or navy skirts that came down to just above the knee, white socks that were generally better preserved than those of the young men, black plastic shoes, and white blouses. Their hair was worn in straight bobs and not permitted to touch the collars of the blouses.

Bom kicked Ute under the table. "Look at that one!" he whispered "Isn't she something else?"

The young woman was about sixteen, had a delicate but perfectly proportioned figure, huge eyes with long lashes, and a bashful smile. She was the closest thing to perfection that Ute had ever seen and she was surrounded by young men who behaved like buffoons. "Do you know who she is?"

"You mean you don't?" Bom asked in amazement.

"Should I?"

"That's Chiang, Lup Law's daughter."

The color slowly drained from Ute's face.

* * *

Captain Lup Law rolled his pen between his fingers as if rehearsing a conjuring trick. The action betrayed the practiced cold attitude of the rest of his features. His daughter sat in one corner of his office sobbing. In another corner stood Tanait, her twin brother. The young man was bamboo thin, almost to the point of emaciation. *You would think I don't have the money to feed him.*

"No, Father, no! I can't do it. No!" Chiang sobbed.

Lup Law brought his attention back to his daughter. The captain had arranged for Chiang to see the doctor at the hospital that morning. She had come to her father's office instead. "Listen to reason, Chiang," he said in a subdued near-whisper. "It would ruin everything—"

"What are you talking about? I love him and I will not kill his baby!" Chiang yelled.

Lup Law closed his eyes and took a deep breath. "It's not killing," he said in a soft voice. "The baby has not yet been born. It has no life of its own until it's born."

"Not according to the Abbott," Tanait said.

Lup Law turned his attention to his son. "The Abbott? You went to the Abbott?"

"Yes. We asked him. He said that an unborn child has already experienced the transmigration of the soul and so to kill it would be a sin. It would break the Buddhist precepts."

Lup Law looked hard at his son and then sighed. He was beaten. He could not be seen in public encouraging his daughter to get an abortion, not when the Abbott at the temple had declared it to be a violation of the Buddhist moral code. "All right," Lup Law said, his voice now projecting. "If that's what the Abbott has said, then we'll keep the child."

Chiang looked at her father blankly for a moment before realizing that she had won. "Thank you, Father." She bowed to him, a smile beginning to grow on her face.

"Now, you go home and get some rest. I have work to do here." Lup Law followed his daughter to the office door and watched as she walked down the hall toward the stairs that led to the ground floor. He turned back to Tanait.

"This did not involve you," he said.

"I didn't want you to make a public mistake," Tanait said.

"You don't achieve a position like mine by making mistakes." Lup Law moved to the window, watching as Chiang emerged from the building and climbed into the back of a pedicab beside Ute.

CHAPTER TWO

The boy at Chiang's breast was strong and determined. Ute had named him Wanlop after an uncle of whom he was particularly fond. Wanlop had ruled Chiang's life completely for all of the nine months since his birth. Like his father Ute, Wanlop demanded everything and gave nothing. He seemed to ignore her once he was satisfied too, like his father. And he was beautiful like his father, fair and handsome with a slight wave in his black hair. She both loved and hated him. Most of the time she was a mother loving and caring for her child. There were times, however, when she was in a darker mood, when she would have smashed him if she'd had the courage. But she had no courage, at least not that kind. What she had was a face to save, and a father who watched her constantly from a distance hoping she would lose it.

Chiang carried the child across the cool wooden floor to the side of the house. She looked down through a wall of one by twos arranged like bars between the hardwood floor and the roof. Outside, working on a tractor engine, was Ute, leaning his back against one of the stilts that held up the house. He was slightly out of her field of vision; she could see only his hands fumbling with the machine. But she knew he leaned against the stilt, the damaged one, because that was his place.

Ute was no farmer. Lup Law had given them the land and the house as a wedding present to prove the point. He knew that Ute could not work the land, that he would fail, and that when he failed Chiang would understand her mistake. But she understood that long before Ute even had a chance to fail. Two days after they were married he spent the night in a local brothel. After that he took her when he wanted her without preliminaries and often violently. Then he would leave her alone for days at a time. He wasn't even there when Wanlop was born.

To make matters worse, Lup Law was actively ensuring Ute's failure by making certain that none of the village folk assisted them in any way. Ute lacked the money to hire migrant workers and so the two of them worked the fields alone, the baby strapped to Chiang's back or lying on a blanket in the shade. Their rice harvest was meager even though the others had a good year, and their mangoes rotted in the trees for want of pickers.

Ute responded to this by drinking and by further abusing her. Once, in a rage, he had taken an axe to one of the stilts supporting the house and had stopped just short of serious damage. Now he leaned against the stilt whenever he was home, as if to remind her that things could collapse at any moment. Only the child seemed safe. He never touched Wanlop, either in anger or affection.

Chiang heard a curse and the hands below her threw an engine part halfway across the yard. Ute stood up and emerged from beneath the house. He was shirtless and Chiang noticed that his skin was beginning to surrender its fairness to the sun. He was becoming a peasant farmer, if only in appearance. Her husband lit a cigarette and then walked slowly over to retrieve the offending part. He cleaned the dirt off and then went back under the house, this time to sleep in the hammock that hung there.

Chiang's eyes did not follow him but lingered on a spot just above where the part had landed. There, through the trees a few hundred meters away, was the house of the *farang*, the white man who called himself Jep. He was young with gold hair and green eyes, and he was the object of much interest from the young women, especially those who were looking for a way out.

A young American Peace Corps worker had come to the town ten years earlier to teach English at the local high school. Before he left, he married a local woman and took her back to America. Now her family received monthly checks and photos of the big house that she lived in. Marry a *farang* and you are instantly rich. This was now the local wisdom.

Jep had been over to visit twice, once when Ute was home and once when he was not. The first time, when Ute was home, Jep came into the yard and asked Ute a lot of questions about farming in awkward sounding Thai. Ute was charming and answered all the questions as if he did know something. Chiang was sure that Jep understood less than half of what Ute had said and was in no position to judge her husband's knowledge of agricultural matters. The encounter seemed to encourage Ute and he even took the little books about Jesus that Jep offered as a gift. These he hid away where Chiang couldn't find them.

On the other occasion, Jep had come seeking Ute when her husband was gone. Jep had strolled into the yard wearing a green shirt made from cloth sewn by village weavers, their local trademark being two ornate one-inch-wide horizontal stripes that ran the length of the fabric. The shirt was beautiful, but it looked strangely out of place on a *farang* body. Over his shoulder, Jep carried a cotton bag made by one of the tribes in the mountainous north end of the country. The bag was light brown and had thin stripes in a darker shade of brown that ran the length of the bag and blossomed into wide fringed tassels at the bottom. Each of the seven or eight tribal groups had a distinctive design and Chiang struggled to remember whose design this was, but could not. Again she thought it looked out of place over a *farang's* shoulder, but then Jep did not dress like any of the tourists she had seen in Bangkok. Jep was out of place, she decided, out of place in a Thai village.

"Is your husband here?" he asked.

"No," she said.

"Oh." He seemed unsure of what to say next. "Is he, perhaps, in town?"

"I don't know."

"He didn't tell you where he was going?"

"No."

"Oh." Jep paused. His eyes scanned the area around the house, not the property itself but beyond where the neighbor's houses were.

He's checking to see who is watching, Chiang thought, but he can't tell. The neighbours can watch from well within their homes, from where they are not visible. But they can see him standing in the sun in the middle of the yard. And they are watching, all of them. And they will tell my father.

"You have a good strong house," he finally said.

"It's old."

"But strong."

"Not so strong."

"Did he tell you when he would be back?"

"No."

"When did he go?"

"Two days ago."

"Two days ago?" He seemed amazed at this.

"Yes."

For a while Jep said nothing. He shuffled a bit and adjusted the strap on his tribal bag. She could see that the sun was beginning to bother him. *Why doesn't he step into the shade?*

She glanced back into the house. Wanlop was awake but he seemed content to play with a bit of cloth. The child took no notice of her. She turned back to Jep.

"I was hoping to ask Ute some questions about the gem trade," he said. "About the people who polish the stones in all those little shops in town."

"He's not here."

"Yes, well, I'll come back when he is." Jep smiled his good-bye and turned to leave.

"Ute doesn't know much," Chiang said. "He's never done it."

"I thought pretty much everyone in this town had a working knowledge—"

"Not him. He was a soldier, then a policeman, now..." She gestured to the field behind the house.

"Oh well then, I'll go ask someone else." He smiled. "Thanks."

"What do you want to know?"

He looked at her curiously, studying her. "Have you done it?"

"No, but some of my friends at school quit to go and do it. They had to. To survive. You can survive if you work hard."

"What kind of wages do they earn?"

"That depends on how fast you are. If you work fast and long hours you can earn a hundred *baht* or more a day, but most people make about half that."

"Fifty *baht* a day?"

"Yes."

"For a full day?" He seemed amazed at this.

"Yes, if they aren't fast. If they are ordinary."

"Fifty *baht* a day," Jep said shaking his head.

"Everyone wants to be fast. Those who are fast can earn a hundred *baht* in eleven or twelve hours. A person can live on a hundred *baht*. At least until their eyes go bad. They hope things will get better before that." She studied the beads of sweat forming on his forehead. "Why don't you come under the house out of the sun? You'll get sick if you stand out there like that."

Jep seemed uncomfortable with the suggestion, but before he had a chance to respond Wanlop began crying.

Chiang went to the child. "He's hungry," she said from inside the house.

"Well, I'll be on my way then," Jep said. "I'll watch for Ute, and when I see that he's home, I'll come visit again."

Chiang watched him leave from inside the house while the child nursed. It was the last time Jep came over, though she occasionally met him on the road or saw him in town. His interests had shifted from farmers to those who worked in the gem trade.

* * *

The young rice plants hugged the earth like a tartan green mist. In the distance, contract laborers, their torsos clothed in American second-hand long-sleeved shirts, were busy pulling up the young rice plants for transplant to another field. It was a familiar sight, a calming sight. It was the reason he came here to pray each day at dawn.

Familiar also was the sound of a small two stroke motorcycle screaming somewhere behind him. Jeff didn't bother to look. It was probably just some kid showing off his latest acquisition, a hot 125 cc Kawasaki, water-cooled, noisy, and fast. It was coming closer, ruining the tranquility he sought. *It will pass,* he thought, holding his eyes firmly on the fields before him. But it did not pass. It stopped a few feet behind him.

"*Khun Jep khrap*?" said an unfamiliar voice. "Jep" was what the Thais called him because they had trouble pronouncing the "F" sound at the end of a word.

He turned to see a young man, his head covered in what looked like a brown ski mask. He held a handgun. Before Jeff could react, a bullet tore through his neck to the right of his Adam's apple and a second entered just below the bridge of his nose.

The man calmly tucked the gun into his pants and drove off. In the distance, the laborers began running toward Jeff. The first to arrive stripped him of his watch and his wallet; the second took his shoes.

CHAPTER THREE

"Sixty," said Sam Watson as he stirred his morning coffee. "Sixty," he said again. He set the spoon on the table and stared at it. He had stopped adding cream to his coffee several months ago, but still found himself stirring the cup. A habit. *Maybe they're right. Maybe you start slipping at sixty.* The toast before him remained untouched. Another habit. Another bit of evidence for the prosecution. He got up each morning and made himself toast and then didn't eat it, at least not until later in the day, by which time it was cold and unappetizing. Then he forced himself to eat it as a form of punishment, or so as not to waste food, as Jeff would say. He looked at his watch. Nearly ten. The mail should be in.

He got up from the table and walked to the mirror in the hallway of his apartment. It reflected a freckled balding scalp fringed by blue-gray hairs that nearly matched the color of his eyes. The eyes were unaided by lenses, a testament to good genes. But the image that looked back at him was slightly ridiculous. A friend had given him a wine-colored bow tie during his combined birthday and retirement celebration three days earlier. Sam tore the offending accessory from his neck and dropped it into the garbage. "I'll tell him it got caught in the blender," he said aloud. He opened the top button of his shirt, watched as the white gray hairs on his chest began slowly rising to fill the cavity. He did the button up again.

Sam arrived in the lobby just as the post woman finished putting the mail in the boxes. "You're running late today," he said.

"Monday," she said and left him fiddling with the lock to his box.

It yielded two items; a late birthday card from Janet, his daughter, and an aerogram from Jeff in Thailand. The card he ignored, knowing that it would contain nothing but a signature.

The aerogram he opened immediately.

> Dear Dad,
>
> Sorry it's been so long since I've written. These days there doesn't seem to be much time for that kind of thing. I'll try to do better in the future.
>
> I have been busy trying to track down local people who claim to have made a confession of Christ through Bible correspondence courses. One of the Christian broadcasting stations sent out a list of all the people who are studying their material in our area. It's not as easy as you would think. A lot of these folks have been studying the Bible through the mail for years but they never go to church or try to find other people with a similar interest. When I show up, they either pretend that there's been some mistake and deny that they've ever received the material, or they say that they've decided to be Buddhist after all. One guy was a little more honest and told me that he believed but that his parents would disown him if he ever went to church. So that's where it stands. We have all these people

studying the Bible but they're afraid to go to church.

I've also been spending a lot of time talking to the people around here who work in the sweatshops polishing gems. I really feel for them. It's piecework. They spend all day, sometimes up to sixteen hours, grinding and polishing these little sapphires in dimly lit rooms. At most they might take home fifty baht ($2.50) for their efforts. But the guys who own the shops are driving around in BMWs and Mercedes and getting richer by the minute. And the weird thing is that the workers accept this. I try to teach them a bit about justice from the biblical perspective, but it's hard.

Well, again I'm sorry for not writing more often. Take care and HAPPY BIRTHDAY!

Your Loving son, in Christ,

Jeff

Sam shook his head, tucked the card and the aerogram into his jacket pocket, and went out the revolving doors into the cool damp air.

It wasn't raining but it had been, almost constantly, for the past three days. Dry patches had appeared on the sidewalk along Nelson Street and it looked as though the sky might clear up before the end of the day. Might. When he first arrived in Vancouver around Christmas some thirty-five years earlier, there were a lot of "might-clear-up" days. But, during his first six months in the city, there were only six days of real sunshine. He nearly packed up and moved back to Saskatchewan.

Sam approached First Baptist Church from the north, from the side where all the interesting aspects of its architecture were hidden behind a brown stone wall. No glory here, he thought, just parked cars. He could see the morning joggers struggling around the roof-top track on the YMCA building next door. Most of them were forty plus, over-weight, and attempting to pay for past sins. You choose your method of payment. His own choice was to walk everywhere, if he had time. It was less painful but a good deal wetter and it only stabilized the problem. The excess still clung to his body in all the wrong places. He didn't care, or rather, he cared, but not enough.

The back door to the church stood between the two buildings. He passed through and down the corridor leading to the church office. One side of the passageway was brick, the former outside wall of the old church. Recent renovations had added a counseling centre and eliminated the covered parking spots of the pastor and his staff. Now they, too, were rained upon when they scurried from the main parking lot to the church building. Never again would a dry pastor preach to damp parishioners. Sam smiled. Dr. Nevil McKay, senior pastor at First Baptist Church, had wavy red hair that reacted to the damp weather by pulling itself into tight little curls. One could tell the relative humidity by looking at Dr. McKay.

Sam found the door marked "Church Office" and opened it. The receptionist, a matronly middle-aged woman with a deteriorating blond perm, peered myopically at a file card. She sighed and looked up at him.

"May I help you?"

"Yeah, I have something for Dr. McKay. Can I give it to him?"

"Well, Dr. McKay is working on his sermon at the moment. He doesn't like to be interrupted when he's doing that, you know. I'd be happy to give whatever it is to him later if you..."

Sam was quite willing to agree to this when McKay, dressed in an immaculate light brown wool suit and with his hair attempting a red afro, suddenly appeared at his office door.

"Is that Sam Watson?" he asked with professional enthusiasm. "Well, well, Sam, it's been over a month hasn't it?" And with that he ushered Sam into his office, leaving the receptionist to puzzle over the handwriting on the file card.

Nevil McKay's office was an exercise in symmetry. His ancient oak desk was located one-third the way from the back wall. His chair, one of those modern backless things designed for better back support, was half way between the desk and the wall. The only two other chairs in the room, both ancient high back executive desk chairs, were at ten o'clock and two o'clock with the centre of the desk at six o'clock. The room was not wide, so this meant that the chairs were uncomfortably close to the desk. The walls were hidden behind two massive bookshelves that went from the floor to the ceiling. They seemed to contain exactly the same number of books. The rest of the room was dominated by a beautiful Persian rug that stopped just short of the wall on all sides. Could one order such an item made to measure?

The only things in the room that defied the symmetry

were the open Bible, a note pad on the desk, and Dr. McKay's hair. "A bit of moisture in the air today?" Sam said with a grin.

Nevil McKay sighed, "To tell you the truth, I'd remove it all if I thought the membership would accept a minister with a shaved head. Ah well, such is life." He gestured to one of the chairs. "Have a seat, Sam, have a seat. I take it you got another letter from Jeff?"

At the airport, before Jeff got on the plane, he had made his father promise to go and personally hand each of his letters to McKay when Sam was finished with them. Sam agreed in the emotion of the moment and now resented it.

"It's pretty brief," Sam said, handing over the aerogram. "Sounds like he's busy."

McKay quickly read the letter. He shook his head. "He's got a hard ministry there," he said. "It's not easy when there's so little response."

Sam shifted uneasily in his chair.

McKay smiled. "You know, Sam, it might surprise you to learn that most believing parents don't want their children to go to the mission field, either. Nobody wants a member of the family to be halfway across the world in some strange and potentially dangerous place for years at a time."

"But he's not accomplishing anything. That's what bothers me. I mean, even assuming they needed to be converted, and you know how I feel about that, he's getting nowhere fast. And I'm not for one moment fooled by this mock positive attitude stuff that he keeps putting in all his letters. Nobody's going to tell me that beating your head against a wall for three years doesn't give you some kind of headache."

McKay smiled again. "Like father, like son?"

"What do you mean?"

"I seem to remember a conversation we had...what was it? Five weeks ago? Six weeks? Anyway, the last time you got a letter from Jeff. You were upset about your upcoming retirement and you were reflecting about your career in the police department. You told me the thing that bothered you the most was the feeling that you hadn't really accomplished anything. That in your thirty-three years as a police officer, things on the street hadn't gotten any better, but were worse."

"Yeah, well, you have to keep on plugging. You never know. You might make a difference in some kid's life or stop some poor fool from doing something really stupid." Sam felt the hollowness of his response.

McKay said nothing.

Sam threw up his arms in frustration. "Look Doc, I'm not against religion. I'm really not. I've seen it turn some people's lives around. It's a good thing in small doses. But I've also seen it take people who were making a meaningful contribution to society and turn them into... Did you know that Jeff was at the top of his class? He was going to be the best damn cop this city has ever seen! Not a duffer like his old man... But he just packed it in and went to Bible school."

Sam didn't continue. He knew he was repeating himself. Every meeting he'd had with McKay had been a variation on the same theme. McKay believed in what Jeff was doing but Sam didn't. McKay was a believer in the absolute necessity of this Gospel stuff and Sam wasn't. They didn't share a common basis for their thinking so they wound up playing broken records for each other.

"Look, Sam, about once a month we have a meeting here when people get together to pray for the missionaries and discuss what they're doing. There'll be a lot of people who think highly of your son and would love to meet you. Why don't you come along? The next one is tonight in the room across the hall."

Sam caught and held McKay's gaze. "You know, Doc., if you take an old trout out of the stream and throw it on the shore, it starts to smell bad pretty fast."

McKay smiled. "Don't worry about it, Sam. A lot of them have been wanting to meet you for quite some time. I think you'll feel welcome."

* * *

Ute had been dreaming; that he knew. But dreaming of what, he couldn't remember. He felt the way he always did after waking from a dream, a slow dawning awareness of reality. Reality, this time, was the breathing of another person; not a familiar rhythm. Someone new was beside him on the mat. He slowly drew himself up and looked at her, a bit surprised that she was still there. Usually they left him before he woke.

This one was young, very young. They had told him fifteen but from the moment he saw her he doubted it. Fourteen maybe. Thirteen likely. He rolled slowly off the mat, picked up his cigarettes and a mosquito coil, and walked out the door and down the steps into dawning light.

Ute felt his bare feet mix with the cool dust around the house. He lit the cigarette and drew on it, its smoke mixing badly with the after-taste of cheap whiskey. He then quickly lit the mosquito coil, for already they were beginning to gather. It had been a bad year. The mosquitoes carried hemorrhagic fever. Seven or eight children had died from this already and the season was not over yet. Though the disease was not often fatal in adults, it was painful and inconvenient. Sometimes it lasted as long as two weeks.

He placed the smoking coil at his feet and looked around him. He was on a farm a few kilometers south of Takli, a place Ouan had inherited from his parents and used for parties. Ute could see the communication dishes on top of Takli Mountain to the north, a remnant of the Vietnam War when American forces were stationed there. He'd been at another remnant the night before, an old nightclub built originally to service American soldiers. It still had faded posters of American rock groups and a jukebox with American records on it, though some of them skipped. It didn't matter. No one went there for the music. The place was now known for virgins, or very young girls at any rate, and that's where Ouan's tastes lay. Ute had gone along for the ride and asked for the oldest girl. Now he wasn't sure they gave him what he'd asked for.

Ute briefly considered waiting for the girl to wake up so she could make him some breakfast, but then he thought better of it. He went back up the stairs, quietly gathered his shirt and his bag, and went under the house where he'd left his motorcycle.

There it stood, a 125 cc Kawasaki—water-cooled, cherry red, noisy fast, and expensive. He had bought it on a whim three weeks earlier with money from a loan shark in Nakhon Sawan. The loan shark thought Ute was still a cop. There was no way Ute was going to be able to make even the first payment so the machine was a ticking time bomb. Add Lup Law into the formula and you had a truly dangerous situation. It was time to get out, to disappear. Chiang had a rich father. She would survive.

He started the bike, knowing that the roar would likely wake the girl above him, and sped out from under the house toward the road. As he turned onto the highway, he caught a glimpse of her standing on the top step with the sheet wrapped around her. He opened the bike up and screamed into town at 115 kilometers per hour.

Ouan was at his usual place in a local restaurant sipping Pepsi and eating rice porridge. He was obese, unusually so for a Thai, because he liked everything fried in pork fat and ate a lot of it. He grinned at Ute as his friend came through the door. “Have a good time last night?” he asked.

Ute raised his eyebrows.

Ouan laughed. “Nice little piece, that one.”

Ute threw Ouan the keys to the motorcycle. “It's parked outside,” he said. “Look after it for me. I'm going for a long walk. Be back in a couple of hours.” Ute watched the look of amazement spread over Ouan's face. “A little reward for last night.”

Ouan grinned. “Sure thing, Ute.”

“See you later,” Ute said and walked out the door. He knew Ouan would spend the next few hours racing around the countryside, and that he would still have the keys in a few weeks' time when they came looking for the bike. A bit of bad karma.

Ute walked the two blocks to the train station and bought a ticket for Hua Hin in the South. It took the clerk a few moments to look up the fare. It wasn't a common destination for the people of Takli.

* * *

It was Sam's plan to arrive late. He reasoned that, if he entered the room about fifteen minutes after the meeting was scheduled to start, he could avoid a lot of embarrassing small talk. But Sam prided himself on his promptness. He found himself in the church fifteen minutes before the event and was, therefore, forced to hide out in the washroom adjacent to the meeting room. From there he could monitor Dr. McKay's opening prayer, Bible reading, and brief homily while he combed his hair and straightened the wine colored bow tie he had rescued from the garbage.

When it appeared that Dr. McKay's homily was winding down, Sam knocked timidly at the meeting-room door. He was admitted by an elderly woman who appeared slightly confused by his presence, but nevertheless managed to direct him to a chair in the corner of the room. This put him in the outer ring of two circles of chairs and made him plainly visible to everyone. He smiled painfully, folded his coat, and placed his hands in his lap.

"And so we are reminded that even Paul, in his own ministry, was constantly dependent on the prayers of the church, of the believers, as he went about evangelizing the people of Asia Minor. So then, as we hear these stories of the work of our missionaries, let us always keep in mind that it is our prayers—our petitions to God on their behalf—that help to keep those missionaries where they are, announcing the news of the love and grace of God to those who have never heard. Let us pray."

It was not Dr. McKay who prayed but rather an elderly woman across the circle from him. Nor was she the only one. Several others followed suit while Dr. McKay himself remained silent except for nearly inaudible comments like "Yes, Lord," "Amen," and "Praise you, Jesus." In this respect he was not much different from many of the other twenty or so participants because, while most were content to merely nod their agreement with the various prayers, many were like the pastor and seemed to need to affirm the prayers vocally. Finally, after about ten minutes, no one seemed to have anything else to pray and the room fell silent. Dr. McKay looked up.

"Well, I'd like to introduce all of you to a special guest who has come to meet with us tonight." Dr. McKay gestured in Sam's direction. Sam smiled and nodded to several people around the circle. "Sam Watson is the father of Jeff, who most of you know has gone out from this church to minister the Word of God in Thailand."

"I have prayed for your son nearly every day since the day he left for Thailand," the woman said as she poured Sam a cup of coffee after the meeting. "I have prayed not only that he would be successful in his missionary work, but also that he would grow closer to God. After all, God doesn't really need our help, does he? But he chooses to let us do it so that we might be obedient."

She looked normal enough, Sam thought, a shade over five feet with a perm of tight gray curls and a kindly face. Her teeth were her own and in good shape too. No mean feat for a woman who was obviously over eighty.

“My husband and I served for a brief time in China before the war. He was a surgeon and wanted to follow in the footsteps of Hudson Taylor, but physically he didn't have the stamina. We had to return home after only four years.” The woman's eyes took on a look of profound sadness, so much so that Sam would have comforted her had he known what to say. But she recovered. “So we became prayer warriors, the two of us, until Percy's death a year ago,” she said and then smiled. “Now I soldier on without him.”

“Well, I'm sure Jeff appreciates every good word you put in for him,” Sam said after a pause. The woman smiled at him and then turned to serve someone else.

Sam looked at the Styrofoam coffee cup in his hand and stirred the liquid vigorously. Nothing changed. What was black to begin with remained black. He set the lip of the cup against his mouth and tipped it cautiously as if trying to avoid irritating a canker. At the first taste he winced. Styrofoam cup, Styrofoam coffee. He needed that just about as much as he needed this meeting. He began looking for an end table hidden in some corner of the room where he could quietly abandon it.

“Mr. Watson?”

The woman who had called was now moving towards him from about half way across the room. Behind her he could see the ideal place to stash the Styrofoam. He moved forward.

“Hello, Mr. Watson. I'm Lena Harwood, head of the mission committee at this church.”

“Hello.”

Lena Harwood was younger than most of the people in the room, perhaps in her late forties. Her dark brown hair was frosted with gray and worn in a short easy-to-care-for style. She dressed with taste but also a degree of defiance, a defiance that came with wealth or intelligence, or both. Sam decided it was probably both. The light brown suit she had on would have been acceptable in any office environment but it also would have stood out. The pockets were at odd angles, the buttons were deliberately mismatched and the accessories drew attention to themselves.

"I think you're uncomfortable in here," she said softly.

"You don't exactly look like you fit in yourself."

"I don't, but coming to these things is one of my responsibilities. I believe very much in missionary work but..." Then she whispered, "These prayer meetings always tend to be such geriatric events." A thin smile of resignation spread over her face.

"I was wondering why there weren't more young people."

"Not much here to attract them, I'd say." She gestured to the Styrofoam cup in Sam's hand. "Even Denny's across the street has better coffee than that."

Denny's did have better coffee, marginally. At least it was served in a decent cup. They had both ordered cheesecake, with Sam taking the lead. Cheesecake was an old vice.

"Aren't you worried about what those old folks are going to think about us walking out together like that?" Sam said.

Lena looked at him curiously and then smiled. "Are you worried about my reputation or your own?"

"My reputation isn't the kind that needs protection. I just wondered how all those elderly parishioners are going to react to the attractive female head of their mission committee stepping out with an unchurched fellow like myself."

"Well, firstly I doubt if anyone noticed and secondly, even if they did they'd probably give me the benefit of the doubt." She carefully cut into her cheesecake and balanced a bit of it on her fork. "I and my family are something of a fixture at that church. I was born, raised, baptized, and married in that church. So was my husband—and you can add buried to his list."

Sam waited a few seconds before responding to this. "How long has he been gone?"

Lena set the fork with the cheesecake down on her plate without tasting it. "I'm sorry. That was a bit glib, wasn't it? It's only been a few months, actually, but it was a long time in coming. Bowel cancer. He was a lot older than I am, almost twenty years. I'm afraid I'm still getting used to being the youngest widow in the church."

"Any kids?"

"Two. Both in medicine at UBC. Cathy is in pre-med and Cal is in nursing."

Sam raised his eyebrows.

Lena laughed. "Cathy has always been the studious one. Her real aim is research, not clinical practice. Cal is not as much of a one for books, but he likes helping people. He was at Dick's side for most of the last few months of his life, and not just because it was his father. He would do that for anyone."

"Wait a minute," Sam said, "Cal is a friend of Jeff's isn't he?"

"Well, yes, I guess you could call it—"

"Because I remember Jeff bringing a young man along

once when we were meeting for coffee. And the kid was going to go into nursing."

Lena nodded. "That would be Cal. And, yes, they are friends, but it's really more of a mentoring relationship. Jeff's almost ten years older, and before he went overseas he was a leader in Cal's youth group at church. So it's that kind of friendship."

"So you have a kind double relationship with Jeff," Sam said. "Both as the head of the mission committee and as the mother of one of the kids in Jeff's youth group?"

"Yes, that's right. I'm very fond of your son, Mr. Watson."

"Sam. Call me Sam."

She lifted the cheesecake to her mouth and then put it down again. "All right, Sam. Now you tell me something about the rest of your family."

Sam shrugged. "Two kids. Same sex and order as yours. My daughter's a travel agent and lives in L.A. She's already been married and divorced twice. No kids. The second guy was an American which sort of explains why she's in L.A. I don't see that much of her. She gets all these free airline tickets but can never find the time to get up here and visit her old man. And Jeff... Well, you know about Jeff."

"And your wife?"

"You haven't told me much about your husband. Just that he was older than you and died of cancer."

Lena smiled. "All right. Dick owned an insurance company, which was already a fair size before he married me. I was a dental assistant at the time but I quit as soon as we got married. Dick was a workaholic, but I managed to slow him down a bit. He loved me very much and took good care of us. He also gave the church about a third of its budget. He was very keen on evangelism and led half his senior management staff to the Lord. They're all very loyal to him and to me. I don't think we've replaced a single man or woman in the front office in over five years. He left me with a lot of money and a lot of emotional support both in the company and in the church." She gestured to him. "Your turn."

Sam sighed. "My problem is, I can never decide whether I'm a divorcee or a widower. I met and married Alice back in Saskatoon before I ever had any idea about being a cop or moving out here. Before that I was in the army. I got in just before the end of World War II and I didn't see any action. That really annoyed me, so I stayed in the army for a while hoping that something would come up. When it didn't I got out, and a few months later the whole Korean thing started to happen. Impeccable timing." He balanced a piece of cheesecake on his fork and studied it for a moment before slowly putting it in his mouth. "Anyway, I tried business and was in the process of doing that when I met Alice. I never could stand being cooped up in an office. Still hate paper work. The problem was that's exactly where Alice wanted me to be." He shook his head. "Her parents were all right-wing free-enterprise conservative Christian types. They didn't like me much." He pointed at Lena's cheesecake. "You're not eating."

"I'm listening."

"You can't do both?" Sam asked with a smile.

"Fatal flaw."

"Okay." Sam put another spoonful in his mouth. "Anyway, my poor attitude at work got me canned so I suggested to Alice that we move out here. Things were a lot better on the West Coast at that time and we didn't have any kids yet, so she agreed. When we got out here, I couldn't find anything that suited me for the first few months and Alice, who managed to get secretarial work right away, began to get impatient. Then the police department started recruiting, and by then Alice was just about willing to have me do anything, so I signed up. She saw it as something I could do for a few years and then leave and go back into business. The trouble was, I liked the work. It appealed to my self-image or something, and I was finally getting some of the action I missed in the army. We had a couple of kids and managed to hold things together for about twenty years."

Sam stopped and gestured to Lena's cheesecake. "I'll pause so you can have a bite."

Lena smiled and put a small piece of cheesecake in her mouth. She chewed, swallowed, and put down her fork. "Continue," she said, pressing a napkin to her lips.

"Well, the trouble with being a cop is you can't really talk over your work with your wife. You see a lot of ugly things and sometimes it really gets to you, but it's not the kind of thing you want to bring home and unload on her. You can't come home and tell her about the little kid you've just seen smeared all over the road or some particularly gruesome murder, so what you do is you talk those things over with your fellow cops but hold your tongue at home. After a while, there's a whole part of you that she just doesn't have access to, and sometimes the lack of communication is just too much. I think that's part of the reason she wanted me to get out. Anyway, one day she just came in and said she wanted a divorce. I can't say I was surprised. She moved out, filed for the divorce, and three weeks later was drowned in a boating accident." Sam shrugged. "I suppose technically I'm a widower but it feels like I'm a divorcee. Either way, you lose the other person."

"So now with your daughter in L.A., Jeff in Thailand, and your wife gone, you're pretty much on your own?"

"Well, I've got my police friends, but no family. I didn't want to retire."

"Ever thought of going out to Thailand to visit Jeff?"

"He suggested it once or twice. The thing is, I don't have all that much cash. I've never been much good at accumulating the stuff, and I bought that stupid condo in the West End at the worst possible time." He shook his head. "I could have got it for fifteen percent less if I'd waited six months. But I wanted to be near Stanley Park, you know, and everything else for that matter. It became something of an obsession. I get those every once in a while. So I blindly went ahead and bought the thing, which means I'm more or less forced to live on my police pension. I'm all right as long as I don't make trips to the Orient."

"Do you want to go?"

Sam eyed Lena Harwood carefully before answering. He knew the cost wouldn't be anything to her. But his pride wasn't quite down to that. "I suppose I have some interest in what it's like over there, but the truth is, I'm really much more interested in getting Jeff back here."

Lena did not respond to this. She played with the remaining cheesecake on her plate and then put the fork down. "Well, if you want to go, you let me know. I'll get you there."

"I couldn't repay you."

"I don't loan money, Sam."

CHAPTER FOUR

The postman squeezed his motorcycle between the idling cars and made his way to the intersection, where he found a dozen or so other motorcycles straddling the white line. The traffic light at Rama Four and Sukhumwit was one of the longest waits in Bangkok. The concept of rush hour traffic had faded in the Thai capital. In the minds of most of Bangkok's population, the distinction now was between daytime and nighttime traffic. During the day, traffic congestion was continual and rush hour only added a few minutes to what was already an intolerable wait. Even at night things could be pretty bad depending on where you were.

Most of the postman's fellow motorcyclists were racing their engines in anticipation of a fast start, but the postman had another problem. He needed to get to the far left so he could turn on to Sukhumwit. There was a small gap between two Honda step-throughs and so he forced himself into that space. Both riders gave him an angry look, but they made the adjustments necessary to let him in. Instead he went through the space and right out into the traffic where he made a quick left, narrowly avoiding a collision with a flatbed truck. The other riders blasted their horns at him, but he knew they secretly admired his courage. If you wanted to get anywhere in Bangkok in a hurry, you had to take risks, lots of risks.

His destination was only a few blocks down on Sukhumwit but now, almost as soon as he entered the street, the traffic came to a halt again. This time he knew there were no traffic lights in front of him, just more congestion. He followed a number of other motorcyclists off the street and onto the sidewalk. They rode single-file past aluminum carts where fried bananas and guavas were sold. Two blocks further down, he turned off the sidewalk into the small lane that led to his destination. Free of traffic, he opened up the bike and raced the fifty meters or so to the courtyard that contained the offices of the Siam Outreach Society.

The courtyard was an oasis from Bangkok's noise and grit. In its centre a large, well watered grassy space was punctuated by trees and children's playground equipment. Almost every time he had come there children were playing—mostly white children—but today there was only the intermittent spurting of an automatic watering system. He stopped, dismounted, and carried the telegram into the building closest to the gate.

Dr. Philip Eaton, medical director of the Siam Outreach Society, was huge by Thai standards. At six foot three and 240 pounds he dwarfed the people he worked with. An old rugby injury had left him with a permanent limp and no comfortable way to get exercise. He gained weight every time he returned to his native New Zealand on home assignment and then lost it again every time he came back to Thailand. Something about the Thai diet did this but he wasn't sure what. It wasn't a lack of carbohydrates because he ate a lot of rice. Perhaps it was a combination of the mangos, papaya, and guavas that he loved and the Thai sweets that he hated. He ate few sweets and only when it was necessary for reasons of etiquette. Dr. Eaton resolved to research the issue when he had more time, but at the moment there were more pressing concerns.

He read the letter again. The doctor who had written was Thai, at least by birth, but he had grown up in L.A. and was now an American citizen. Still, he was born in Thailand and that might help the mission get around the restrictions the Thai Government had placed on medical visas. The problem was the man's faith. He was a young Christian, a believer for less than a year. As a surgeon in the hospital, he would automatically be in a position of spiritual authority. Dr. Eaton's task was to tactfully suggest the man get some theological training.

There was a timid knock on the door.

"Come in," he said.

Dhara, his secretary and the person who kept the office functioning when he and Stuart were up-country, slowly opened the door. She was dressed in a loud blue and white outfit that, like most suits worn by female office workers in Bangkok, tended to emphasize the hips. She smiled apologetically and handed him a small light-green envelope. "This just come for you," she said in English though he spoke Thai fluently.

"*Khop khun khrap,*" he said in response, taking the envelope. Their conversations were almost always bilingual with each using the other's native language, a source of endless amusement around the mission. Dhara closed the door and went back to her work.

He opened the envelope. It was from Banmi, Jeff Watson's station, but it was written in Thai and it was not from Jeff. He read the message twice before calling Dhara.

"Get Stuart on the line quick!" he said in English.

"And don't stop trying until you get through!"

* * *

Stuart Haddon drove and prayed simultaneously as a matter of habit. On this day the prayers came in short bursts punctuating long periods of numbness. Another man down. Last time it was a motorcycle accident; this time a shooting. He knew nothing more than that. The telegram said only that Jeff had been shot and was in the Banmi hospital. His office had been unable to get through to the hospital by phone, a problem with the lines. Such problems often took days to solve. So he got in the pickup and made the half-hour drive to Banmi.

It went quickly, but now that he was in the town, things slowed. The pedicab in front of him carried no passengers but the aging driver was, nevertheless, laboring to his destination. Stuart had long since given up trying to guess people's ages in Thailand. He was often out by as much as twenty years. The pedicab driver was old enough to get a pension in England, of that he was certain. The old fellow seemed disturbed about Stuart's presence and kept glancing back over his shoulder at the lime-green Isuzu pickup. But he did not speed up or move over and, in the end, wound up going to almost exactly the same place that Stuart was going, a small gathering of pedicab drivers just outside the hospital compound. They began to talk about Stuart, gesturing toward the hospital as they did so.

Stuart parked the pickup as close to the hospital's main entrance as he could and got out. His slim frame tended to stoop, though he was not overly tall and he bore a superficial resemblance to Irish playwright

Samuel Beckett. The author, however, wore his hair in the ragged brush cut whereas Stuart glued his hair to his scalp with Brylcreem.

Two policemen, in dark brown uniforms with large caliber handguns strapped to their waists, were smoking on yellow wooden benches under a canopy outside the door. They regarded him casually. "Are you here because of Mr. Jep?" one of them asked.

"Yes."

The officer nodded and then continued smoking as if the matter were closed. But when Stuart went through the doors into the hospital, both officers got up and followed him.

Inside the hospital, staff were busy dismantling the morning's out-patient clinic. A few patients were still sitting on long wooden benches waiting to see a doctor. Stuart caught the eye of one of the duty nurses, who immediately came to him.

"Are you here for Mr. Jep?" she asked.

"Yes."

"He's in the operating room. His people are waiting down there." She gestured to a corridor of the main reception and out-patient area.

Stuart entered the corridor and immediately recognized Pastor Sanit with a dozen or so of the local Christians standing outside the operating theatre talking with a doctor. The pastor looked up as Stuart approached. The look on his face told Stuart that it was already too late.

"When?" asked Stuart.

"Just a few minutes ago."

The two Thai police officers were not far behind Stuart. They glanced at the doctor and his expression told them what they wanted to know. They turned to Stuart. "You are Mr. Jep's boss?" one asked.

"Yes," Stuart said. It was simpler than trying to explain how the society worked.

"We are catching the man who killed him. We will have him shortly. You will have to come down to the station and press charges." The officer spoke in basic Thai.

"Yes, well, I'll need to talk to my superior first. Did you say the man was already in custody?" Stuart's Thai was good, the product of nearly twenty years of living in the country.

"We know who did it. We will have him soon," declared the officer, not switching from his simplified delivery. "You should come to the station."

"I will come to the station when you have him," Stuart replied. "At the moment I want to talk to the doctor in private."

"Yes, of course," said the second officer, speaking normally. "We will send someone to get you when we have the man in custody." With that the two officers turned and left.

Stuart turned to Pastor Sanit. "I'll go and have a look at the body and then we'd better go someplace where we can talk."

Sanit nodded and said nothing.

Stuart studied the rest of the group and greeted each by name. They were from the small Christian church in Khoksamrong, a twenty-minute drive from Banmi. Most of them had their personal medical histories written loudly on their faces and in the stumps and distortions of their limbs. Leprosy. They had known more pain and humiliation than he would ever know. But they were now Christians, holding on to the faith that Jesus would one day make them whole.

Stuart turned to the doctor, a young man whose discomfort with the situation showed plainly. "Would you please take me to see him?" he asked.

The doctor smiled nervously and then led Stuart into the operating theatre. The nurses and other technicians were busy disconnecting wires and tubes from Jeff's body. One glance was all that was necessary. The lower wound showed that the bullet had passed cleanly through the neck, grazing the spinal cord and coming out the back. The upper wound, however, had hit the upper lip, smashing much of the upper jaw. No open coffin at this funeral, thought Stuart grimly.

"I'm surprised he lived long enough for them to get him in here," the doctor said. "He should have been dead on the spot. But then neither bullet did much damage to the spinal column. The lower one passed to the right and the upper to the left. If we'd had him immediately, we might have saved him, but by the time they got him in here, he had lost too much blood." He smiled apologetically. "His blood type is fairly common in the West. But few Thais have it. We didn't have any here."

Stuart nodded.

"What do you want us to do with the body?" The doctor looked distinctly nervous at having to ask the question.

Stuart studied the doctor for a moment before answering. "Do you have a morgue?"

"Yes, of course. But you see this was a murder. A lot of the people who work here are afraid of demons." The doctor's embarrassment was evident.

Stuart nodded. "Keep the body cool and I'll make sure we have him out of here as quickly as possible."

"Thank you, Sir."

Stuart turned away from the doctor and made his way back to Sanit. "Do you know anything about this?"

Sanit had been one of the mission's first converts in Thailand. His face was lined both by age and by the years he had spent sitting in the sun with a begging bowl. "He was watching some workers transplant the rice early this morning. He liked to pray for them while they worked, after he finished his other prayers. Someone came on a motorcycle and shot him. A neighbor of his brought him here in a pickup truck."

"Do you know who shot him?"

"No. But Jep must have made some enemies. It was a hired killer."

"A hired killer? How do you know?"

Sanit smiled grimly. "It's the kind of thing you know from the way things are done."

Stuart nodded. "Where is the neighbor? I'd like to thank him."

"He's gone to the spirit doctor. To have his truck cleansed."

The two men regarded each other with an air of mutual resignation. "I have to make arrangements to move the body quickly. Can you put together a service for the people here?"

"When?"

Stuart shook his head. "I don't know yet. I'll let you know."

"It doesn't matter. Everyone will come."

"Is there any place around here where I can use a phone? "

"There are many phones, but none of them are working. They say the last rain knocked down the line and no one has fixed it yet."

"Then how did you find out?"

"A friend who worked at the hospital told Bim. He borrowed a motorcycle and came and got me."

"And you sent the telegram?"

"Yes."

Stuart sighed. "I'd better send one, too. Will you wait here until I return?"

"We will stay and pray."

"Thank you."

Outside, in the parking lot, Stuart vomited before climbing into the pickup. The two policemen laughed.

CHAPTER FIVE

The air was humid and hot. Puddles of various sizes dotted the road, and in one of these two small boys played with a paper boat. An open-air restaurant, one that served noodles and soup, stood on the sidewalk next to the puddle. It consisted of a large metal pushcart equipped with a gas stove, a variety of cooking implements, and an awning overhead to shelter the vendor. The vendor herself was a portly woman who was mother to the two boys playing in the puddle. Two square tables with peeling surfaces and patched umbrellas overhead completed her establishment. At these sat two men, both slurping noodles and reading newspapers. Neither paid any attention to the other, or to the young man in new Adidas running shoes and designer jeans who was walking by the restaurant.

The woman noticed him. He had given her a wink as he passed by. She knew him as a sometime friend of her husband's and a man who never did anything that she knew of to earn his fancy clothes. She watched him walk a bit further down the street and enter one of the larger gem polishing sweatshops.

Inside the door the young man, known to his acquaintances as Nak, stopped to watch the gem polishers work. Most were too focused on what they were doing to notice his arrival. They were hunched over spinning wheels grinding tiny sapphires into usable shapes. Nak scanned the room until he found what he was looking for, an attractive young girl, perhaps fifteen, who had recently left school to learn the gem-polishing trade and make her own way. She was faring badly, as most did at the beginning. That made her easy prey. In a week or two she would be so frustrated that the idea of getting involved with someone who obviously had a little money, like himself, would be attractive, even if she was a bit uncomfortable about where he got the money.

Nak made his way to the room at the back. It was enclosed in glass and had a large teak door. Inside the air conditioning was on full. He would have knocked but the room's occupant saw him coming and opened the door. He was ushered in quietly.

The thick glass that enclosed the room and the hum of the air conditioning made speech inside inaudible to anyone in the sweatshop. Still, both men felt compelled to speak in subdued tones.

"Have you completed your task?" the old man asked.

"He's dead," Nak said. "I think you know that already."

"Yes, but how did you know?"

"I waited in the hospital."

"You shot him and then went to the hospital to see if he was dead?"

"No one saw me do it. At least no one was close enough to be able to recognize me." Nak laughed. "And I had a legitimate reason to go to the hospital." He pulled up his pant leg and revealed a gauze bandage. "I burned my leg on that motorcycle's exhaust pipe as I was getting away. Nice bike, by the way, but I prefer Scramblers. Can't think why you wanted me to use the Kawasaki. Anyway, what's the big problem? You made arrangements with the police?"

The old man studied Nak's features for a moment and then nodded slowly. He took eight crisp new 500 *baht* bills from his shirt pocket and handed them to Nak.

"This is only four thousand," Nak said. "I told you my fee was eight thousand."

"You told me that the job would cost me eight thousand and after that you said that I would have to make arrangements with the police. Those arrangements cost me four thousand."

"But..." Nak stopped himself. The old man sat down in front of the large Buddha shelf, which served as a backdrop for his desk, and gestured for Nak to leave. Nak knew he was beaten. He bowed before the old man, who appeared to take no notice, and then left.

* * *

The knock at Sam Watson's door was light and Sam probably wouldn't have heard it had he not been in the hallway, preparing to go out. Sam opened the door.

"Mr. Watson?"

The man who stood before him looked familiar but Sam could not remember who he was. The man himself didn't help. He stood at Sam's door looking extremely uncomfortable and flustered, like someone caught red handed at the scene of a crime.

"Yes, may I help you?"

The man shuffled and then changed his facial expression several times as if trying to find the right one. When nothing seemed suitable, he looked down. "I'm sorry, Mr. Watson," he finally said. "I've never had to do anything like this before." He paused. "I've come to talk to you about Jeff."

At the mention of Jeff, Sam knew immediately who the man was, or at least what he was connected to. The name was still missing, but Sam knew the man was some kind of local administrator with the Siam Outreach Society, Jeff's mission. His presence meant that something was wrong overseas.

"Is he all right?"

The man slowly shook his head. "He's been shot. I'm sorry."

"Shot? By a gun? Is he...?" Sam didn't finish the final question. He read the answer in the man's face, turned around, walked back into his apartment and lowered himself slowly onto the sofa. He untied the shoes he had just put on and took them off. For a moment he stared at them, then he looked up and saw that the man had followed him into the room. "When?" he asked.

"Early yesterday morning."

Sam's eyes strayed to the man's hands. They held a small wine colored Bible.

"He was shot near a field by a man wearing a ski mask and riding a motorcycle. The neighbours got him to the hospital all right, but he needed a transfusion and they didn't have one available."

Sam stared at the man without answering. "Jeff," he said finally.

The man shifted his weight from one foot to the other several times. "I'm very sorry, Mr. Watson," he said finally and began opening the Bible.

"Don't."

The man closed the Bible. Sam looked away to the window where the rain beaded and the sky grayed. After a few moments he took the pen from his shirt pocket and held it out to the man. "Write down your name and number and I'll call you."

Sam turned back to the beaded rain and the gray sky. Behind him the man left his name, number, and Bible.

* * *

Captain Lup Law wore his BMW like a royal vestment. He imagined it flowing around him, adding grace to his every movement. He knew it spoke volumes to all who saw it and today he wanted to make their ears ring. Today he would drive it around and around the town and just smile at people. Today he would begin to rid himself of the one great embarrassment in his life. Things were coming together beautifully.

* * *

For a while Sam thought that he might have imagined it, that in reality no one had actually come to his door and told him that Jeff was dead. But now, two hours later, he remembered every instant of that visit and it had none of the fleeting images that made up dreams. It had been dream-like in a bizarre way, of course, but such things often were. The man wasn't used to giving that kind of news and Sam wasn't used to receiving it. Why should it be strange that neither had handled the situation well? He had been in the man's position a number of times during his career, when he'd had to tell people of the death of someone close to them. He'd had some practice, but it was never easy.

Sam had got almost no information from the man. He'd made a career out of asking questions, but the moment Jeff's death had been established all of that had deserted him. He knew only that Jeff had been shot near a field by a masked man riding a motorcycle, and that they had taken him to a hospital where he had died due to loss of blood. He did not know where the body was, what they planned to do with it, who was in charge of the investigation, whether or not they had caught the assailant, what they expected of him, and a host of other important details. What he did know was loss, terrible loss, and he had no idea what to do with that. A black hole had taken up residence in his chest.

Then it dawned on him that he needed to call Janet, but what would he tell her? Better to get more information first. He found the man's name, William Stevens, and reached for the phone just as the first sob took him and held him long and deep.

* * *

The stove over which Chiang cooked was a metal bucket with a molded ceramic piece inside. This held the coals and also served as a base for the wok in which she stirred the vegetables and small bits of chopped chicken. Beside it stood an electric hot plate that she almost never used except to heat water when one of her guests wanted tea. It was a wedding gift. Another electric appliance, a rice cooker, stood in the corner. It was gathering dust. She only used it when others were around.

She had never been through a time of isolation like this. There were days when no one came around at all. The neighbours watched her like vultures waiting for her to die, forbidden to make contact with her by her father. She could not go to the market because to do so would leave the house empty and send out a beacon to all the thieves in the area. They all knew she was alone and would strip the place of anything valuable the minute she was gone.

Ute had only been home four days in the last three weeks and those were the only days she managed to get to the market. But he hadn't been back in over a week. There had been an argument. Chiang had suggested that he sell the new motorcycle. They could use the money to buy some things they needed. Ute became angry and drove off.

Since then she had been dependent on Lek, her younger sister, or Tanait. Both would go to the market for Chiang when they could, but they were sometimes kept at home by Lup Law. It was a calculated thing, Chiang thought as she stirred the food. Her father was allowing one of them to come just often enough to keep Chiang from starving.

Chiang began listening for Wanlop. The child was asleep in the next room, but about due to wake. As she listened she realized that the dog was growling, but quietly, as if frightened. She went to the side of the house and looked out. Two police officers with guns drawn were slowly approaching the front of the house. She looked around quickly and saw that there were at least three more coming from other directions. What has he done?

She slowly stepped out onto the porch at the top of the stairs where most of the officers could see her.

"Where is your husband, Chiang?" one of the officers asked.

"I don't know," she said. "He hasn't been around for

over a week." They know this, she thought, Why the pretense?

"Did you know that the *farang* was murdered?"

She was startled. "Jep? When?"

"Come on, Chiang, you must have known."

"How could I know? My father won't let any of the neighbours talk to me!"

"Surely that's not true," the officer said smiling. "Anyway he was murdered by a man wearing a mask and driving one of those new Kawasaki water-cooled motorcycles. You know, like the one your husband's been telling everybody he won in a lottery. Only he didn't because no lottery in the area has had one of those as a prize. We checked."

Chiang was shocked. "And you think Ute shot Jep?"

"Yes, either as payment for the motorcycle or perhaps out of jealousy. We're not sure of the motive at this point."

"Jealousy? What are you talking about?"

"Well, we know the *farang* visits you when Ute is not home. And we know that Ute knew about this, too. He was quite upset about it. So we have two possible motives already."

Chiang was angry. "*Khun* Jep came over here exactly once when Ute wasn't home. He was looking for Ute, actually. He was here for less than ten minutes and he stood right over there in the middle of the yard and never came closer. What would Ute have to be jealous about?"

The officer smiled. "Well, that's your story, of course. We have orders to bring him in and to take you and the child over to your father's house."

"My father's house?"

"That's right. You're sure you don't know where he is? It would certainly make things much easier, and we will get him eventually."

Chiang said nothing. She glared at the officer until the man turned away. Then she went in and got Wanlop.

CHAPTER SIX

Stuart Haddon drove the Isuzu pickup into the parking lot, gathered the newspapers lying on the seat beside him and made a quick dash between the vehicle and the air-conditioned offices of the Siam Outreach Society. Inside, he paused to let the receptionist unlock the door between the inner and outer offices and then walked right past her to Dr. Eaton's office. He knocked.

"Please come in," said a voice from within.

Stuart entered and closed the door behind him. Dr. Eaton looked up at him through an expression of grim fatigue and then smiled. "Hello, Stuart," he said. "Now what are they saying?" He asked gesturing at the papers.

"More of the same, really. They're looking for some ex-police officer who they say was jealous of the attention Jeff was paying to his wife. The wife denies this but the newspapers have dug up several people who say they've seen her and Jeff together. Here, look at this one." He passed the paper to Dr. Eaton. The headline asked the question, "Murdered missionary and wife of ex-police officer sleeping together?"

Dr. Eaton shook his head. "Oh, boy."

"And that's not the worst of it," Haddon said picking up another paper. "The editorial in this one is all about how this case serves to illustrate Christian morals and sexual mores."

Stuart opened the paper to the page in question and handed it to Dr. Eaton. The doctor took a few moments to read the column, blanching as he did so. "Is there even the remotest possibility that Jeff was paying attention to this woman?"

"Well, it wouldn't be the first time one of our single men went astray, but, in Jeff's case, I don't think it's likely."

"Still, we'd better be prepared for the possibility."

"I suppose." Haddon was silent for a moment. "I think this whole thing is connected to Jeff's social work."

"Social work? Oh, you mean his concern for gem workers." Dr. Eaton thought about this for a moment. "Surely he wasn't that aggressive."

"It isn't the reality that matters, it's the perception."

Dr. Eaton let himself sink slowly into his chair. He shook his head. "Missionary martyrdom, now there's a concept for you, all full of glory and honor...What if it is simply a mistakenly jealous husband or a merchant concerned about his bottom line? Is he still a martyr then? Or maybe just some kind of victim of circumstance...I just want him back, Stuart."

"We all do."

The two men regarded each other for a moment.

"How are they taking our silence?" Dr. Eaton said.

Stuart shrugged. "Admission of guilt pure and simple. And they're saying we don't want to prosecute because, if we do, other terrible things about Jeff's conduct and the behavior of Christian missionaries in general are sure to come to light."

"It's funny how they're so intent on getting us to prosecute when they don't even have the suspect in custody."

"I think they expected to have him by now. That's the other thing, you know. Sanit thinks it's some kind of set-up. Apparently there wasn't much love between this fellow and the local police captain. Sanit thinks the whole thing might have been fabricated just to get at this guy." Stuart shrugged. "But, then again, the man has disappeared. Why run if you haven't done anything?"

"Unless you knew someone powerful was going to try and get you. Anyway, it doesn't have to be true in order for someone to believe it. He might have killed Jeff because of what he believed and not because of any real situation. The point is that it's been done, we've lost one of our missionaries and if that isn't bad enough, we have major damage control on our hands. If something like this gets out of hand we could all—and by all I mean more than just the SOS missionaries—we could all be gone permanently."

Stuart pursed his lips. "So you think we should just take our losses, sit tight and pray that the damage will be minimal?"

Dr. Eaton nodded. "The Thai press will probably tire of this in a few days, especially if we don't add any fuel to the fire."

"Then there's something else we need to pray about."

"What's that?"

Stuart squirmed uneasily in his chair. "What do you know about Jeff's family back home?"

"Not much. I think he's the only Christian, if I remember right. He never talked about it much to me. Apparently they've agreed to let him be buried here." Dr. Eaton paused to consider the implications of this. "Oh, I see. You're worried that they won't understand our decision not to cooperate."

Stuart nodded. "Yes, I'm worried. His father is a police officer. A real law-and-order type, apparently. He might not be very understanding."

Dr. Eaton considered this for a moment. "Who's our representative over there?"

"Bill Stevens."

"Oh," Dr. Eaton's face took on a look of frustration. "I think our budget's going to have to spring for a fairly lengthy long distance call. Do you want to do the honors, or shall I?"

* * *

Tanait was grateful for the tinted glass that shrouded the back seat of his father's BMW. He hated the car, knowing that Lup Law had bought the vehicle with proceeds from the sale of heroin. If Tanait was forced to ride in the car, at least the tinted glass would give him some anonymity. The irony was that his father had bought the car so equipped because he had seen important people in Bangkok riding around in similar chauffeur-driven vehicles. Lup Law's original intention was to have one of the officers drive him around in the same way. But that, of course, would mean that the captain wouldn't be seen and he definitely wanted to be seen. So now Lup Law drove the car himself and his passengers, at least those in the back seat, were the invisible ones.

Tanait could, however, see out and right now his father was slowly driving past the temple grounds. It was midmorning. By now the monks had eaten and were going about their various tasks. Everything looked so serene, so right. In a few months Tanait would join the *Sangha*, the community of monks. He would devote his life to studying the *Dhamma*, the glorious wisdom that the Lord Buddha had brought to the world 2500 years earlier.

* * *

Where the sea met the land at Hua Hin was a white sandy place. It stretched for over three kilometers with a famous temple at one end and a vacation home for Thai royalty at the other. In between developers and speculators bought and sold, driving up the price of land beyond the range of all but the wealthiest Thais. The tourists, tired of the filth on the beach at Pataya, were finally coming and there was a lot of money to be made.

It amused Ute to watch them attempting to brown themselves in the Thai sun. Stupid people, he thought. Why would anyone want to be brown? The Thais never lay in the sun during the day. They knew the value of fair skin. But those who had it naturally did not seem to value it at all. Some of the European women even went topless laying there like corpses on the sand pretending that no one would notice, or thinking they lacked sophistication if they did, or perhaps hoping they would. Why was it only the ugly women who did this? They were certainly no match for the women at the club, even with their big white breasts.

The men were even funnier, overweight, wheezy, and sunburned. When they went to the club at night the girls had to put cream on them so they wouldn't be too uncomfortable and would spend money.

Ute shifted his weight in the hammock and turned to look at Bom. His young friend was in another hammock a few meters from him. He did not look well, his nose was stuffy, his eyes were often watery, and he coughed a lot. At the moment, Bom's right hand hung lazily and a half-smoked joint of northeast pot smoldered between its fingers. He had a Walkman on his chest and was lost in its music. In the few short days since his arrival, Ute had learned that this was how Bom spent his days. At night he made arrangements for the girls at the club.

Bom had been pleased to see Ute arrive. Things were starting to get competitive and he needed a little protection. Who better than an ex-police officer, especially one as tall and strong as Ute? They would work as a team. He would teach Ute the trade.

Ute studied his stoned friend and thought about the way things had been when they were both monks. Bom had followed him around constantly, hoping that Ute would help him escape from the monastery. When Ute finally found him a job at a motorcycle shop, Bom promised to repay him. Three months later Bom disappeared.

Ute later found out that Bom had gone to Bangkok to work the streets. There, the young man had been told, was where the real money was, the money to buy the motorcycle he wanted so badly. But Bom acquired little money selling himself on the streets of Bangkok. What he did acquire was a rudimentary knowledge of the English language and soon he began using it to make arrangements for others. Bangkok, however, is a dangerous place to do that kind of work, especially when one is working alone. After one particularly bad beating, Bom decided to relocate to Hua Hin. The beach resort's speed was much more to his liking and after a few months he wrote Ute a postcard. "Hello from Hua Hin. Making lots of money. Come visit," was all it said.

Ute laughed at the post card when he read it and threw it in the garbage, but Chiang rescued it and tacked it to one of the support beams of their house. It was a place she wanted to go if they ever got the money for a vacation, she said. Then she should get the money from her rich daddy, he told her, but he left the card on the beam.

Now Bom had his motorcycle and he drove it recklessly and stoned. But Ute would keep a clear head, and he would learn the trade.

* * *

When Sam Watson called Lena Harwood and asked if he could meet with her, he had in mind another coffee at Denny's or something similar. What he got was an invitation to dinner at her house in Shaughnessy. Lena even sent one of her company's employees to pick him up, a young man, pimply clean, who kept a snap-flapped Bible on the dash of the company Buick. The boy said little but breathed Listerene, sweated Old Spice, and fingered the pine-tree-shaped air freshener at every traffic light.

The Harwood place wasn't as big as he expected but it kept big company. The surrounding houses averaged six large bedrooms and harkened back several well-preserved generations. They filled their lots well but left room for the hired landscapers to play. In this context, the Harwood home looked like some poor Victorian child forced to dress like an adult. A miniature version of the homes around it, it nevertheless managed to radiate youth and liberalism, a quality that the surrounding sequoias seemed poised to restrain.

The boy in the Buick dropped him at the curb, and before the car door was completely closed, Sam heard a cassette drop and the beginnings of a guitar intro. “Had enough of this morbid silence, have you?” he said under his breath as he watched the vehicle recede.

He was in no hurry to make his presence known but he could also think of no good reason why he shouldn't. Denny's he could handle. This he wasn't so sure. He studied the house for a moment and then resigned himself to the task before him.

The doorbell was exactly that, a bell. It rang once, loud and clear, and decayed slowly. Lena took a long time to answer but the bell was still ringing when she did.

“That's quite a chime you have there,” Sam said by way of greeting.

Lena smiled. “Isn't it though? It was a gift. Dick knew this Turkish family who lived out in the Maritimes. They had a family business of making cymbals and bells for various uses. Once struck, this one will ring for over a minute. Here, let me take your coat.”

Sam removed his coat and handed it to Lena. “Thanks,” he said, and followed her into the house. The living room was dark, not through any absence of light but rather because of color choice. A lot of dark wood accented with green and deep gold. The only bright objects were the paintings—West Coast water colors, each of which had its own small light. The lights hung from a system of tracks on the ceiling. It took Sam a few moments to realize that these were the only sources of light in the room.

“Would you like something to drink?” Lena asked.

“Drink?”

“I'm afraid I only have beer or wine, but I have a pretty good selection of those.”

"Uh no, I don't think so."
"Coffee?"
"Uh...please. Yes. Coffee would be nice."
"It'll take a few minutes. I can do espresso or cappuccino if you like. I'm afraid I don't have instant."
"Just regular drip would be fine, thanks."
With that Lena went into the kitchen and left Sam to sort out his strategy. He lowered himself slowly onto a dark green leather sofa and tried to avert his eyes from the paintings. When this failed he got up and crossed to a bookshelf in the corner and pretended to study its contents. But he soon found himself reading the jackets and trying to remember the names of books he'd read by the same authors. Anything but deal with the problem at hand.
"Do you like to read?" Lena said, coming up behind him a few moments later.
"Yes, I do," Sam said.
"I'm afraid it's not much of a collection. I don't accumulate books. I tend to loan them permanently, or at least that's the way it seems." They were both silent for a moment. "Can I ask an old question without getting an old answer?" Lena said.
Sam studied her face for a moment before answering. "Sounds a bit tricky."
"How are you doing?"
Sam smiled. "I'm supposed to come up with a new answer for that?" He walked back over to the sofa and sat down. "The one person in my life that really mattered is dead. Oh, he's been gone for years, but now he's dead. He won't be coming back. My daughter's been trying for three months to find an empty space in her schedule so she can come up here for a few days and

comfort me. The Baptist church down the road keeps sending over cookies, the Siam Outreach Society wants me to forget the whole thing, and all I want to do is go over and see where they buried my son."

Lena studied him for a moment. "Why don't you come into the kitchen and talk to me while I set the table?"

Sam followed her into the kitchen. It was large, even huge. It contained every imaginable piece of culinary equipment, including a machine to make bread, one to make espresso and cappuccino, and one to make fresh pasta. There were two microwaves. The coffee was quietly hissing through its filter in a modest Philips brewer that looked strangely out of place beside the big brass cappuccino maker. Off to one side was a large eating area complete with a solid oak table large enough to seat ten comfortably. It was then Sam realized that there was no dining area off the living room.

"Like to eat in the kitchen, do you?" he said.

"Always did, and so did Dick." Lena carried plates and some cutlery to one end of the table and then gestured to the wall separating the living room from the kitchen. "When we first moved in here that wall didn't exist, but there was one here and here." She gestured to the floor on either side of the table. "So you see we'll actually be sitting in the original dining room only now it's part of the kitchen instead of the living room. I never did like carpets in an eating area, especially when you have small kids, and ours were small when we moved in."

"Well, I always appreciate eating in someone else's kitchen. It kind of makes you feel included, if you know what I mean."

There was a small electronic sigh. "Coffee's ready,"

Lena said and went to fetch it.

On Sam's plate lay the remains of a chicken thigh, leg, and breast, a pile of artichoke petals, overlapping puddles of sauces and a pineapple rind. The wine glass by his right hand had been filled and drained several times. Before him loomed the specter of chocolate mousse and, try as he might, he could not find room for it.

Their conversation had made the rounds of church politics, police procedures, old cop stories, insurance claims, and family memories. Sam talked about Alice and Lena talked about Dick, but it was the Dick of years ago, not the one who had just died. Jeff was mentioned only in passing, as if the early mentioning of his death was all that was necessary. It had all been a glorious bit of escapism, but it was drawing to a close. His body, which had eagerly welcomed the food, was now beginning to work it into small hard lumps. He became silent and watched as Lena made labored adjustments to her posture.

"You know, before Dick died, I had a lot of time to prepare," she said. "We could all see it coming a mile off." She paused, waiting for Sam, but he said nothing. She smiled. "So I read...you know all about coming to terms with grief, with losing someone else. It was kind of morbid in a way. All the books were aimed at people who had already lost someone close. They were addressing an event that had already happened. But, in my case, it hadn't happened yet. Dick was still there suffering, growing weaker day by day but still there. Still talking, laughing, loving me.

I was reading all these books trying to figure out how

I was going to cope with losing him. It was a selfish act, really. Instead of focusing on Dick's pain I was anticipating my own. But, you know, that's exactly what he wanted me to do. He even sent Cal out to buy me books that he'd heard about. A very good man, my husband, which almost made it harder in the end."

Another long pause. Sam fixed his eyes on the dessert that neither had touched, and then he let them go out of focus.

"Anyway," Lena said, "all the books were in agreement about one thing. Grieving is a process that you must go through. You have to grieve. So after he died I went through the family albums and cried over the old photos a couple of dozen times. I wept with my family members and our friends. Visited the grave. Read all his old letters...thanked God in my prayers for the time we had together...all that kind of stuff." She looked at Sam until he looked back up at her. "I'm still doing it, Sam, because I'm not through it all yet. It's only been about nine months. But I know it's been good, painful but good. And I know I've had every advantage when it comes to being able to grieve properly.

Go to Thailand, Sam, go and see where they buried him, go and talk to the people who worked with him, who loved him. Go see the people he served, get to know them. Go and grieve and don't worry about the money."

CHAPTER SEVEN

Ute ground out his latest cigarette in the half-coconut shell that wobbled on the table. He took a drink of Singha beer and watched for a few moments as the last bit of smoke trailed off amid the rhythmic shadows that played across the tabletop. Sometimes it was almost as much fun to watch the shadow as the source. As he did so he allowed himself to guess the movements she was making up there on her little dance platform. If his mood was particularly good, this might even arouse him, but not tonight. Tonight he had learned that the police were looking for him back in Lopburi province. Not that they were likely to find him, but he was concerned nonetheless.

Bom, who sat across from him at the table, was coming down from his cannabis afternoon, coughing and hacking as usual. He needed a few more drinks before he would start to talk and move around. Then he would begin to circulate among the foreigners and rich Thais with his little business cards, cards that described in small print everything that one could hope to find in a place like this. It was hard to read the cards in the club's dim light but one didn't need to read much in order to know what they offered.

Ute looked up at the woman dancing about ten feet from him. She wore nothing but a few strategically placed bits of Thai silk. A recent arrival from a village somewhere in the northeast, she had already sent money back home to help her family. Bom had a friend who did the recruiting, and Ute and Bom handled things at this end. She had learned her lessons well, one of his more enjoyable students, and now she needed only his occasional protection. A lucrative arrangement. He smiled at her and lit another cigarette.

* * *

Sam spent most of the seventeen-hour flight between Vancouver and Hong Kong chewing nicotine gum because they wouldn't let him smoke. He did not enjoy the in-flight movie, both because it was stupid, some bored British housewife in a monologue about escaping to Greece, and because he was too far away from the screen to see it properly. Neither was he interested in reading the various magazines offered to passengers and instead spent inordinate amounts of time searching for holes in the endless cloud cover below the plane.

At the airport in Hong Kong, Sam presented his passport for the first time, the first time a passport of his had ever been stamped. He had possessed one for some sixteen years. He applied for his first when he and Alice were considering a continental vacation to shore up their failing marriage. After that he just kept renewing it, always with the best intentions of going somewhere but never going. *It took the death of my son to put a stamp in that book.*

He told Janet to do everything on the cheap because he didn't want to spend any more of Lena's money than was necessary. The twelve-hour stopover in Hong Kong reduced the airfare by nearly two hundred dollars. It also gave him the chance to take a brief look at the city that had sent so many immigrants to Vancouver. He'd dealt with some of them, and they weren't always desirable. It's easy to be a racist, he thought, when you're always dealing with a people at their worst.

On the way to the hotel, two things struck him. One was the incredible number of people on the street at that time of night, and the other was the way the business signs hung precariously over the narrow roads.

The hotel the airline put him in was as Western as anything in Vancouver, with the exception of the staff, who were all polite Orientals. The room was small but adequate, including a bathroom and cable TV. An investigation of the TV revealed one English-language channel with largely British programming and another that continually ran commercials about where to shop and what to do in Hong Kong.

As Sam got ready for bed, he realized the room was uncomfortably warm. When what looked like a heat-regulating control seemed unable or unwilling to respond to his wishes, he decided to open the window. He was greeted by a rush of much warmer air and a cacophony of strange noises rising from the street below. The air conditioning *was* on. He closed the window, set his alarm for seven hours later and slept on top of the bed.

The cab ride the following morning differed from the first only in that there were fewer people on the streets. *Well, at least I can say I've been to Hong Kong*. Sam remembered a traveler friend once saying that, if he could count hotels and airports, it would double the number of countries he'd been to. *What about flying over some country's airspace?* Janet had already explained that the flight from Hong Kong to Bangkok would take longer because they couldn't fly over Vietnam.

The cab dropped him at the airport, where he checked in and found coffee. He drank it with cream because they served it to him that way without asking. It never occurred to him that anyone would actually do that. He took an aisle seat because he hadn't been able to see much out the window the previous flight and he wanted the legroom.

The Don Muong Airport in Bangkok was new, clean, and had only about a third of the people that were in the Hong Kong airport . He presented his passport and the three-month tourist visa he had picked up at the Thai consulate in Vancouver. Both were stamped virtually without inspection and he was waved through, his luggage unopened.

As he came through the doors leading to the main part of the airport, he looked in vain for someone carrying a sign that read, "Siam Outreach Society." What he did find were a number of company names and a man holding a sign that read "SOS." Sam smiled grimly at the irony of the initials.

"Siam Outreach Society?" Sam asked the man.

"Yes. Are you Mr. Watson?"

Sam nodded. "Now I know why your organization never abbreviates its name in its literature."

"Personally, I wish it would, but the directors aren't comfortable with the idea." The man offered his hand. "I'm Stuart Haddon. I run the non-medical aspects of our activities here."

Sam took Haddon's hand. "The man I talked to on the

phone?"

"Yes. I'm ultimately responsible for the missionary work we do here. That includes what Jeff was doing. He was a great loss."

Sam pursed his lips but said nothing.

"Yes, well..."Haddon gestured to Sam's luggage. "I guess we'd better get this stuff into the truck. I'm afraid you're looking at a long ride."

"A ways to go, have we?"

"The guesthouse is on the other side of town and the roads are always congested."

"The legendary Bangkok traffic?"

"Have you ever been outside of North America before?"

"No."

"You'll see. The truck's just outside those doors."

Haddon began pushing the cart with Sam's luggage toward the door. Sam watched him walk a few paces before following. There was determination in Haddon's stride.

When the door opened, Sam felt the thick heat immediately go right through his clothes. The only thing missing in this sauna was the smell of cedar chips. The odor that replaced it reminded Sam of a suicide he had attended early in his career, breaking down the doors of a locked garage to find an old oil-burning car running and a man lying dead on the floor.

Haddon threw Sam's luggage under a canopy in the back of a pickup. Beyond him Sam could see three rows of traffic, mainly trucks, buses, and taxis. Motorcycles with helmetless drivers were weaving in and out of the lanes. The trucks reminded him of the farm vehicles they had in Saskatchewan in the late forties, big heavy things that had been used to move grain and animals to market. Some of the Thai trucks were dangerously overloaded with cargo rising as high as six feet above the vehicles' side panels. Others had people riding on top of the loads or hanging onto the sides. No one seemed particularly concerned about safety.

Most buses were orange, grossly overloaded and in various stages of disrepair. Here and there Sam spotted a more modern but equally crowded blue bus.

Haddon finished loading the pickup and turned to see Sam studying the orange bus closest to them. "We call them the orange crush. It's mainly people from up-country coming into the city. They may have been riding like that all day." He gestured to one of the blue buses. "Those are city buses. They're usually even more crowded, but at least the ride is shorter."

"What's the passenger limit?"

Haddon just smiled. "Better get in. We've got quite a way to go."

Sam climbed into the truck, closed the door, and immediately wanted a steering wheel, a brake, a clutch, and a gas pedal. Haddon started the vehicle and then shifted down into first.

"I think it would take me a while to get used to shifting with my left," Sam said.

"I never had that problem, being from England, but the Americans and Canadians in the mission seem to get it soon enough."

Haddon eased the truck into the traffic and they began moving along at about fifteen kilometers an hour. Motorcycles passed them, weaving in and out of the traffic and sometimes driving on the grass beside the road. The bikes where all small, averaging 100 ccs, and most were fairly new. About half of the drivers were young well-dressed males with attaché cases strapped behind them on the seat. The other half were a mix of tradesmen carrying tools and materials and delivery men with boxes, often stacked to near-impossible heights behind them. One even had a semi-circular rack with a variety of brushes hanging from it. These swung and swayed with the movement of the bike, but did not fall off. Sam shook his head.

"Principal source of transportation around here," Haddon said. "It's the only thing most people can afford, if they can afford that. Believe it or not, some of them go into debt for years just to buy a 90 cc step-through. Their definition of freedom, I guess." He gestured to one of the bikes attempting to navigate between two buses directly in front of them. "Look at his mirrors."

A young well-dressed and impeccably groomed Thai man was driving the bike in an aggressive fashion. As Sam watched he noticed that the mirrors were not angled in a way that would give any kind of view of the road behind the bike. "What's wrong with him?"

"Nothing," Haddon replied. "He just likes to look at himself while he rides."

"And I thought we had a problem with women putting on makeup as they drove."

A motorized three-wheeled taxi pulled up beside them. It had a black canvas top in the shape of a capsized rowboat with the pointed end towards the front. The driver, who had no passengers at the moment, controlled the vehicle with motorcycle-style handlebars. The taxi was two tone blue and yellow and had a bench seat in the back that could probably accommodate three passengers in a pinch.

"They're called *tuk tuks*," Haddon said. "For the sound that they make. They're cheaper than taxis and okay for short hops, but they put you right out there breathing all the fumes. And you'll get pretty wet if it rains. Tourists usually try them once or twice for the experience and then take regular taxis."

The traffic was now more stationary than mobile. A motorcyclist wearing a brown uniform and a helmet drove by. Sam thought he saw a handgun strapped to his waist but wasn't sure. "Police or military?" he asked.

"Police," Haddon replied. "The military uniform is dark green."

"Pretty small bike."

"They only go up to about 150 ccs here. To get anything larger you have to go to a specialty shop and have them brought in from Japan or the U.S. They're usually second-hand, expensive, and it's hard to get parts. The police tend to use what's available here. They have a few 400 cc bikes, though."

Sam studied the traffic again. "What happens if you have an emergency vehicle in a situation like this?"

"Emergency vehicle?"

"Police, ambulance, fire truck..."

Haddon smiled. "I once saw an ambulance on Silom road with its lights flashing, totally unable to move for half an hour."

Sam considered this. "You're telling me that emergency vehicles don't have the right of way here?"

"To tell you the truth, I'm not sure. There may well be a law to that effect but it wouldn't matter if there was. To yield right of way you have to be able to get out of the way."

The pickup came to a stop. In front of them there was

a line of traffic three lanes wide stretching as far as Sam could see. Some of the motorcycles where spilling on to the sidewalk but even these had slowed to a crawl. Sam looked back. Already the lanes of traffic behind them had filled in to the point where he couldn't see where they had been.

"Now the waiting begins," Haddon said. "At this time of day we may well be able to walk the next kilometer faster than we can drive it."

"And if I were in a police cruiser..."

"You'd be stuck just like everyone else."

Another police officer riding a small motorcycle passed slowly by them on the sidewalk.

"Preferred mode of police transportation?" asked Sam.

"They're a little quicker than a car."

Sam looked a Haddon. "So what did Jeff use when he was here?"

"He uh...Well when he was living in Bangkok...He uh..." Haddon took a deep breath. "Most of the language students just used the bus. There were a few more adventuresome ones who bought motorcycles. I don't think Jeff was one of them. It's been awhile since he lived here, though. He didn't like the city much. About half the missionaries feel that way."

"I can see why."

As he looked at the streets, they seemed to Sam to be curiously modern in the Western sense of the word. Many of the newer office buildings would not have looked out of place in Vancouver. Shop houses were the dominant form of housing, businesses on the ground floor bleeding into living space behind and above. Most of these were light green, tan or blue, and had an oily in-need-of-a-good-paint-job appearance. All the buildings were inter-connected by a kitten-tangle of wires. There were none of the wooden houses on stilts that Sam had seen in postcards and tourist brochures and there was little green space.

About half of the men on the streets looked as though they were businessmen on their way to a job interview. Long dressy pants were almost universal among this group, as were short-sleeved sport shirts, Brylcreemed hair, and dress shoes. Some even wore sport coats and ties.

Sam gestured to one of these. “Air conditioned office?” he asked.

“Probably,” Haddon replied. “You don’t see a lot of Western-style suits outside of Bangkok. There’s a lot less air-conditioning, too.”

The rest of the men fell into one of three groups. The first of these wore service uniforms, either khaki or green and accessorized by black boots and wide belts, sometimes with utility pouches and holsters. Military-style brush cuts were common.

The second group were more casual and diverse in their dress. Shorts and sandals were more common here as were T-shirts and longer hairstyles. These men had a dusty appearance and the clothes were often threadbare and mismatched, but even among this group Sam got the sense that appearance was important. They clearly had limited resources but these men were trying to look their best. There was little of the deliberate casual sloppiness that one saw on the streets of Vancouver.

Buddhist monks made up the final group but there were not a lot of them around. They wore orange-brown robes, shaven heads, and sandals, congregating in the vicinity of Buddhist temples. These buildings were ornate monuments in gold and red. They had tiered roofs that ended with what looked like fingers of flame reaching up towards the sky.

Few women wore service uniforms, so the distinction was between those who worked in offices and those who did not. The office workers were easy to spot because they wore the same kind of office clothes that one would find in downtown Vancouver, only with more uniformity and less variation in style. Pantsuits, or anything else that reflected a more masculine image, were conspicuously absent. Everything was ultra-feminine, shapely, and snug. High or at least elevated heels were everywhere. These women looked hot, uncomfortable, and overdressed. Sam noticed what he assumed was a more cultural style of dress among the second group of women. Many wore a kind of sarong, long pieces of colorful fabric that were wrapped around the waist and tucked in.

"This the part of town where Jeff spent his time while in language study," Haddon said. "We're in the South now, not too far from the port. This street is called Rama Four Road, after the fourth king in the current Thai dynasty." He gestured to what looked like a group of street vendors selling vegetables. "Khlong Toey is behind, probably the biggest slum in the city. I suggest you don't go in there by yourself."

"Pretty rough is it?"

"Can be."

"Did Jeff?"

"Did Jeff what?"

"Did he go in there?"

Haddon waited a moment before answering. "I don't know," he said finally. "I was just an ordinary missionary in Central Thailand when Jeff was in Bangkok. I only came in on business. Jeff was under someone else when he was here."

"Who?"

Again Haddon took his time answering. "Well, let's see. He was out here about seven years. That would put him in Bangkok about '81. That would have been under Dennis Reimer. He's retired."

I'm grasping at straws. I've been in this country less than one hour and already I'm grasping at straws.

"See that building in front of us?" Haddon asked.

They were approaching a three-way intersection. Directly in front was a large three-storey concrete building. It looked to be about thirty years old and government-functional.

"That's the main post office around here. I don't know if you'll have any reason to use it, but there it is anyway." Haddon turned the car left at the T in front of the post office. "And this street is called Sukumwit. The guesthouse is a few blocks down off a lane to our right. If you're taking the bus, any Sukumwit bus will get you there."

"I don't know that I could fit on one of those things."

Haddon shrugged. "It only costs two *baht* to find out. That's pretty inexpensive transportation."

The truck went down a side street, drove about two blocks and then turned into a courtyard filled with tall palm trees, grass and children's playground equipment. Beyond this was a two-story wooden house, well windowed. Haddon parked the truck next to the house. "This is the SOS guesthouse."

Haddon walked around to the back of the truck and began unloading Sam's luggage. Sam followed him. They both picked up bags and carried them into the house.

The entrance gave way immediately to an eating area dominated by a table large enough to seat twenty. Around this buzzed two Thai women with table settings and food. Haddon said something to them in Thai. They both looked at Sam and giggled.

"I told them you were a Canadian policeman who's come to arrest them."

"You've blown my cover," Sam said.

"*Phaw Khun Jep, chai mai*?" one of them said to Haddon.

"*Chai,*" Haddon responded.

The woman approached Sam, put her hands together in a manner not unlike a child's prayer posture, pressed her thumbs against her forehead and bowed forward. "*Sawhadee kha,*" she said.

Sam looked at Haddon.

"She asked if you were Jeff's father and I told her you were. The last thing she said to you was a greeting. Just put your palms together chest height and say 'sa wha dee khap'"

"*Sa wha dee khap,*" Sam repeated.

The woman smiled and went back to her work. As she did so another woman, this one Caucasian, came into the room. Sam judged her to be about fifty. She was slight, almost to the point of looking frail, but there was a bounce to her step that told Sam she was anything but. A middle-aged Katherine Hepburn came to mind. Haddon was about to introduce her when she spoke up for herself.

"Hello, Mr. Watson," she said extending her hand. "I'm Marion Cole. My husband Cyril and I run the guesthouse."

"Pleased to meet you," Sam said.

"We know your reason for being here is not a happy one but we'll do our best to make your stay here as comfortable as possible. If you'll follow me, I'll show you to your room." She started walking down the hall and Sam and Haddon followed. "It's one of our air-conditioned ones, a bit small but comfortable." She pulled a key from her pocket, opened the door to a room about two-thirds the way down the hall, and then handed the key to Sam.

"Now let's see, we're about fourteen hours ahead of you, so for you it must be about seven in the morning. That would make you pretty tired, I would think, especially after all that time on the plane. Supper is in about half an hour. I suggest you come for that, keep yourself awake for another hour or so after the meal, and then go to bed. That will give you a pretty good head start on jet lag."

"Thanks," Sam said. He had not been thinking about sleep but now that Mrs. Cole had mentioned it, he suddenly felt tired.

"Oh, and Mr. Watson?"

"Yes?"

"In Thailand, the custom is to take your shoes off before entering a house."

Sam looked down at his shoes and then at the sock feet of his two companions. "Sorry, I was thinking hotel."

She smiled. "It's all right. I'm surprised Stuart didn't say anything."

Haddon looked slightly embarrassed.

"I'll see you in about half an hour then?" said Mrs. Cole.

"All right," Sam said. Mrs. Cole walked back down the hall. Sam turned and carried the luggage into his room.

Haddon followed him in and they put Sam's bags by the bed. "The bathroom is down at the end of the hall," he said. "It's a shared one, I'm afraid. And don't worry about the *cheechaks*. They're completely harmless."

"*Cheechaks*?"

"Small lizards about the size of your pinkie, a member of the gecko family I believe. They eat bugs and are everywhere in this country. I guarantee that before supper you'll see at least one on your wall."

"Lizards on my wall...right. Okay. Why not?"

"Well, then I'll see you at supper time," Haddon said. "After that, if you feel up to it, we'll spend a little time organizing your stay here."

"Okay, sounds good."

"See you then." With that Haddon left, closing the door behind him.

Sam sat down on the bed and began taking off his shoes. He then removed his bags from the top of the bed and laid down on it. *Cheechaks. Right.*

CHAPTER EIGHT

When Ute failed to turn up to collect his motorcycle, Ouan's first thought was that his friend must have stumbled onto an extraordinarily good time. What else could make him forget about such a marvelous machine? Ouan spent a lot of money on fuel, tried the bike out on every possible terrain, and even managed to pick up a couple of nice young girls by pretending the bike was his. But when Ute failed to return after three days, Ouan became uncomfortable. He began to cut down on the number of times he used the bike and finally parked it in front of his house, throwing a sheet over it.

Now it haunted him. It had a spirit, perhaps Ute's spirit because his friend must surely be dead. It would strike at Ouan because of something he'd done to offend it, or perhaps because of some act of evil he had done in the past. He was never sure if the law of karma encompassed spirits or if they were somehow outside of it. Getting the bike away from the house might be a solution, but he could no longer bring himself to touch it. He thought of calling a spirit doctor to remove or somehow neutralize its power. But to do so would attract a lot of attention; he knew instinctively that would only make things worse.

* * *

The *cheechaks* kept Sam awake until dinner, not

because they were noisy, but because they were fun to watch. The first one appeared about five minutes after Haddon left the room. It ventured out from behind a painting to nab an insect on the wall. Shortly after that another one appeared, this one a bit larger and making a soft clicking noise. It took a run at the first one, chasing it clear across the wall. Both disappeared behind the bureau where the clicking grew louder. After that Sam saw a number of them, mainly feeding on insects but sometimes clicking, chasing, or even mounting each other.

The dinner bell rang. Sam walked down the hall in his sock feet, both wanting slippers and feeling too hot as he was. He made a mental note to watch for bare-footed individuals at supper but he was the last to arrive and everyone's feet were already out of sight beneath the table.

“Mr. Watson, I'm glad you decided to join us,” Mrs. Cole said, rising from her chair.

“I found it hard to sleep with all those *cheechaks* mating on my walls,” Sam said.

Mrs. Cole blanched and glanced quickly down at the man in the chair beside her. Sam assumed he was Mr. Cole. The man met her eyes and then looked at his plate. She turned back to Sam and gave him a tentative smile. “They are rather active,” she said.

There were seven other people at the table. A young couple with an infant sat opposite the Coles. The wife wore a faded cotton floral-print dress with no sleeves. Her hair was blond and cut short on the sides and back; it was too thick on top. She was not looking at Sam but was preoccupied with feeding the child. Her husband, a thin young man with a small purple birth mark on his chin and oily black hair, gave Sam a knowing grin. He wore a plain white shirt with too many pens in the pocket. One of them leaked.

Two slim fortyish women occupied the next two seats. They looked like they belonged to each other. One wore a slightly green ruffled blouse while the other wore a slightly yellow ruffled one. The green lady had dark curly hair with streaks of gray and her friend had straight light brown hair that curled up slightly just before her collar. Both regarded Sam with suspicion.

Haddon came next. Across from him and to Mr. Cole's right sat an older white-haired gentleman with a Freudian beard and mustache. He wore a marine-blue shirt that seemed to have a clerical collar, but the fabric of the shirt was woven and glossy. He regarded Sam with intense interest. "Jeff's father?" he asked.

"Yes."

The man smiled, stood and offered his hand. "Philip Eaton," he said. "Dr. Philip Eaton. I work at the mission hospital about an hour south of where Jeff was stationed." His tone changed and he lost eye contact with Sam. "A sad business, that," he said, his voice soft.

"Pleased to meet you Dr. Eaton." Sam shook the doctor's hand.

"Yes, well, let's introduce the rest of the table, shall we?" Mrs. Cole said, and gestured to the young couple. "This is Tom and Elsa Diwert with baby Ruth. They've just recently come from New Zealand to begin language study here and they hope eventually to work up north among the *Pwo Karen*."

Sam nodded. "Hello."

"Seated next to the Diwerts," Mrs. Cole continued, "are Mary Cortez who comes from New Mexico and has a Spanish American background and June Ashton from Somerset. They work in the South among leprosy patients."

"In a hospital?" Sam asked.

"In a pickup, actually," June Ashton answered. "We travel around doing clinics in the larger towns. We didn't know Jeff well—we were down south while he was in central—but we were shocked and saddened by the news."

Sam nodded.

"You already know Stuart and have just met Dr. Eaton, who also primarily works with leprosy patients, by the way, so that leaves my husband, Cyril. In addition to helping out around the guesthouse, Cyril also teaches Greek and Hebrew at the SOS seminary here."

"Pleased to meet you," Sam said.

Mr. Cole smiled but said nothing, turning his attention back to his empty plate. His pallor suggested a man who wasn't well. It was hard to imagine anyone could be that pale in this climate. He had the head and face of a thin man, but his body and arms were flabby. Thin wisps of grayish-white hair trailed across his scalp, moving in a funny little dance to the rotations of the ceiling fan above him.

He hasn't got the energy to relate to me, Sam thought. "Where should I sit?" he asked.

"Why not there beside Dr. Eaton?" Mrs. Cole said.

"Why not, indeed" said the doctor patting the chair beside him.

Sam lowered himself into the chair and smiled at everyone.

"I'm afraid we don't have anything exotic for you tonight, Mr. Watson," Mrs. Cole said. "The evening meal is usually Western food around here. The missionaries like it that way because most of them get very little Western food at their stations. Things like pasta and potatoes are hard to come by in Thai villages."

"Western food will be fine," Sam said. He studied the table in front of him. There was no pasta and there were no potatoes. There was a large plate of rice, but that was certainly common enough in Western kitchens. A tray of fried chicken, all dark meat, a cucumber salad and a bowl of mixed broccoli and carrots rounded out the offering.

"Dr. Eaton, will you do the honors?" Mrs. Cole said.

"Of course. Oh Heavenly Father, we thank Thee for Thy bounteous offering and ask that Thou wouldst bless it to our bodies' use. We thank Thee also for the safe arrival of Mr. Watson and ask that Thou wouldst comfort him at this time. We pray also that Thou wouldst grant him a deep experience of Thy grace while he abides with us. We ask these things in the Name of Thy Son and our Lord and Savior, Jesus Christ. Amen."

"Amen," echoed the others quietly.

Sam turned to Dr. Eaton. "Can you pray like that in Thai?"

The doctor was about to answer in the affirmative when Haddon cut him off. "No, Phil hasn't quite mastered Jacobean Thai yet," he said with a grin.

The doctor passed Sam the chicken. "Stuart is always needling the older missionaries who grew up with and studied the King James Bible," he said.

"Grew up with it myself," Sam said, taking the chicken.

"Oh, were you brought up in a Christian home?" June Ashton asked.

"Well, What does that actually mean? I went to Sunday school as a child. And we had the usual school prayers and that kind of thing. And we had a Bible in the house, of course. Normal for my generation I think. But no one in our house came any where near the obsession level that Jeff had." Sam paused and looked around the silent table. "It must have been the King James Bible. Until Jeff found Jesus..." He paused at this point, using his fingers to add quotation marks around the name "Jesus." "Before that, I didn't even know there were other versions."

"Translations actually," said Cyril Cole. His voice was reedy and squeaky and seemed to have an ambiance, almost as if he had two sets of vocal cords. "I don't like the word versions because it gives the impression that there might be more than one version of the truth which, of course, is nonsense."

"Is it?" Sam asked.

"Tell Pat that the chicken is excellent as usual," Dr. Eaton said quickly to Mrs. Cole.

"Yes, it is good," Sam said.

After another short silence, Dr. Eaton said to Sam, "Have you decided what you will do first?"

Sam wiped his mouth with his napkin. "Go and see the place where you've laid him, I guess. I'm really not sure. I have to get a bit of a handle on how things work here. Stuart and I are going to go over some of that tonight."

For the rest of the meal the conversation consisted mainly of updates of what was going on in their particular fields of endeavor. For a short while Sam listened to this and asked a few questions but after a while he began to tune it out, becoming more and more aware of his own fatigue. Finally he excused himself and went back to his room. There he collapsed fully clothed on top of the bed and slept, missing his appointment with Haddon.

* * *

Chiang preferred to eat sitting on a mat on the floor, like most Thais, but her father had bought a solid teak table, at a cost nearly double his yearly salary before he had been made captain, and now he insisted that every adult in the house sit around it. The child was exempt because he never ate with the family. Instead he gulped morsels pushed into his mouth by Chiang or one of the other adults, as he ran from one play activity to another.

Tanait was the least comfortable with Lup Law's eating arrangements. Chiang smiled at this. Her brother would not participate in the opulence that Lup Law's position afforded them, much to the irritation of his father. He ate only the most basic of foods, bought all of his clothes at the cheapest place in town, and didn't even own a radio.

"Let's see," Lup Law said counting on his fingers. "I've booked the band, the catering has been arranged, the tables, chairs and tents will be arriving from Lopburi tomorrow and Kwanchai's got the movie equipment coming in from Singburi on Tuesday... Have I forgotten anything?"

"I just wanted a simple ceremony, "Tanait said.

Lup Law looked sternly at his son. "I told you before this is not about you, this is about your mother. The time you spend as a monk earns good karma for your mother. It's not about you."

"Is all this what she wants?"

"I'm a man of prominence in this community," said Lup Law. "People will expect a big party and that's what they're going to get."

Chiang shook her head. In a few days Tanait would experience *buat phra*, his initiation into the Buddhist monkhood. For twelve weeks he would live as a monk, learning Buddhist precepts, chanting ancient texts, meditating, and walking from door to door in the early morning to receive food offerings. His head would be shaved and he would wear an orange robe. All of this he would do to earn good karma for his mother, a Thai custom that had a long history. *What Father doesn't know is that Tanait has no intention of leaving the Sangha after twelve weeks.*

The last person who sat at the table, besides Lup Law himself, was their mother, Dokmai. She was a weak and submissive woman from whom Tanait had inherited his gaunt appearance. She had a slight crook to her mouth, the permanent legacy of a bout with Bell's palsy.

Tanait reached over and gently touched his mother's hand. "I will do this because I love, honor and respect you," he said. "And because I am the only son," he gestured to Chiang and Lek, "I will do this for all three of us."

Dokmai smiled and nodded slowly. In truth she was only Chiang's and Tanait's mother, Lek being the offspring of one of Lup Law's mistresses. When Lek's real mother had died, Lup Law brought the child home to Dokmai. Dokmai said nothing and obediently took the child in, but Lek knew her status in the family was tenuous. She behaved accordingly, deferring to other members of the family at all times.

Chiang looked at her father across the table. He was now using his fingers to extract meat from a chicken bone. It was not the action itself that interested her, but the expression on his face. Despite the tension between father and son he seemed to be enjoying some secret amusement. Chiang knew it was only a matter of time before they all knew what it was. Lup Law never kept such things to himself for long.

"I found out where he got the money for the motorcycle," Lup Law said without being asked.

Everyone looked at him.

"A money lender in Nakhon Sawan, a very rich man. Apparently Ute was wearing his old police uniform when he arranged for the loan." Lup Law smiled. "And he's almost two months late for his first payment. The rich man is not happy." The captain looked at Chiang. "His employees are looking for your husband and the bike."

* * *

Sam's first awareness was of warmth and stickiness, then that he was still wearing his clothes, and finally that he was not at home. He sat up and checked his watch, 6:30 a.m. local time. He had slept twelve hours.

A soft light from the window played with little filaments of dust. Sam looked out on to an empty sun-lit courtyard and then to the parking lot beyond. Haddon's truck was gone. He could hear the muted sound of someone talking coming through the window but it was too indistinct for him to make out the words. After a few moments he decided that whoever it was spoke in Thai. The rhythms were not English rhythms.

The air conditioner was off and a note beside it told whoever was in the room to leave it off when the room was unoccupied. That explained his current condition. He forgot to turn it on before lying down. Sam checked his appearance in the mirror above the bureau. His clothing was now more wrinkled than he was and stuck to him in odd places. He walked to the door and looked cautiously out into the hallway. It was empty.

The bathroom was wall-to-wall and ceiling-to-floor tile. The floor was wet. A showerhead dripped noiselessly from one wall. Along another was a rectangular tank over a meter deep and long and about half a meter wide. This was full of water and had two tin dippers. There was no tub but there was a towel rack and a bottle of someone's shampoo. Sam wiped his feet on the mat provided and walked back to his room. He gathered what he needed for a shower and then returned.

Breakfast was already in progress by the time he reached the dining room, but only Dr. Eaton and the two leprosy nurses were present.

"Well, hello, Mr. Watson," said the doctor. He looked at his watch. "I'd say you've dealt old jet lag a fatal blow."

"Morning," Sam said. "Yes, it's been years since the last time I slept around the clock." He took the seat beside Dr. Eaton. "Stuart's already gone, then?"

"Had a few errands to run. Said to tell you he'd be back around noon."

Sam nodded.

The table had three large bowls on it. One was full of what looked like granola, the second one had some kind of flakes, and there was a steaming bowl of something white in the third. All three of his companions were eating from this third dish.

"What is it?" Sam asked Dr. Eaton.

"*Khaw tome...* Rice porridge. Wonderful stuff. Far better than the stick-to-your-ribs concoctions they serve us back home."

"Only eat it if you're hungry," June Ashton chipped in. "It tends to really fill you up." Her bowl was now empty and she looked satisfied.

"All right," Sam said and spooned some into his bowl. He tasted it. It was a bit thinner in texture than the porridges he was used to and reminded him of salty chicken soup. But when it hit his stomach his whole body sighed contentedly and he knew he'd found what he needed.

All three of his table mates, Sam found out, were heading for the airport. The two women were going home on furlough and Dr. Eaton was picking up a medical colleague at about the same time.

"It's lucky Dr. Eaton was going to the airport at that time," said Mary Cortez. "Otherwise we'd have to use Stuart and I think he gets pretty tired of driving people back and forth to the airport."

"I have my own vehicle, you see," said the doctor. He seemed embarrassed by this. "When my wife took ill we had to spend a few years back home. We took leave from the mission's support system and I worked at a local hospital until her passing." He shrugged. "So when I came back out I had enough money to buy one, and I did. It really has allowed me to accomplish much more." Dr. Eaton looked at his watch and stood up. "We'd better be moving, ladies."

Sam helped load their bags into Dr. Eaton's Toyota

and waved as they drove off to the airport. When he turned back to the house, he found Mrs. Cole standing in the doorway.

"I see you're up," she said.

"Up, dressed, and full of porridge."

"You know that Stuart's out until after lunch?"

"Yes, Dr. Eaton told me."

"What would you like to do this morning, then?"

Sam looked down at the brown oxfords he was wearing, "Well, is there a place around here where I might buy a pair of sandals? I'm beginning to think that bringing these shoes was a mistake."

Mrs. Cole nodded. "Do you remember the way back to the main road?"

"Sukumwit?"

"Yes."

"Yes, I think I can find that. It's just down the lane."

"Well," said Mrs. Cole, "just go out to Sukumwit, turn left and walk about four blocks and you'll find yourself in the middle of an area with a lot of small shops that sell clothing. By the time you walk there they should be open. They're used to tourists so you can deal with them in English if you keep it simple."

All the people that Sam saw on his way to Sukumwit were in open delivery vans, *tuk tuks*, taxis, or on motorcycles. Several of these honked at him as they raced by. At first he wondered if he was breaking a law or something but soon realized it was just a warning to let him know they were coming.

He reached Sukumwit with hot feet and the Hawaiian shirt Janet had given him years ago already sticking to him. He turned to the left and found people. Most of them were either waiting for the bus or setting up food stalls on carts. No one seemed to be shopping and they paid little attention to him. He trudged past them looking for shade and wondering why he hadn't at least brought a hat. There was no shade and soon his scalp began to glisten and then bead.

The shops he passed did not sell clothing. They sold furniture, toys, hardware, even computers, but not clothing. He began to wonder if he'd gone in the wrong direction. He was now nearly at the post office Haddon had pointed out the previous day. He decided to go in and ask them where to buy sandals.

The building was cavernous, not unlike the main post office in Vancouver. There was no air conditioning but high ceiling fans, freestanding fans, and smaller table-top fans were everywhere. Around these buzzed maybe fifty people in khaki uniforms, but there were only two wickets open and large groups of people gathered around each. There was no discernible line, but the people seemed to know whose turn it was. As Sam drew near to one of these groups, he became uncomfortable with by the idea of talking to anyone. He turned around and walked out of the building, his heart pounding. *God, is this what they feel like when they first come over to Canada?*

Then he saw clothing. Shirts, hats, jeans, belts, and shoes were set out under a canopy across the street. They seemed to be right on the street.

Sam looked for a way across. A block down to his left was a skywalk. This looked safer than the intersection. He made his way to it and climbed the metal stairs. The railings were too hot to touch. When he reached the top he found four people sitting on the walkway in the bright sun. First of these was a small boy, perhaps eight, whose legs were unnaturally collected beneath him. He wore a soiled light-blue T-shirt that was several sizes too big for him and red shorts. In front of him there was a bathroom scale and a small metal cup.

Next to the boy was a neatly dressed woman selling what looked like lottery tickets. It took Sam a few moments to realize she was blind. Beside her was another woman holding a small girl. This woman had no obvious disabilities, but her clothes were rags and the child looked ill. They gave no indication of being aware of him. Rounding out the quartet was an old man. His nose and ears seemed to have sunk into his head. Various digits were missing from his limbs and those that remained were either partial or curled and distorted. It was the first time Sam had seen someone with leprosy.

He walked past them and then stopped about the middle of the skywalk and pretended to study the traffic below him. He felt for the coins in his pocket and found three. He walked back quickly and gave them to the man with leprosy, the woman with the child, and the boy with the scale. The boy gestured to his machine but Sam shook his head. "I know how fat I am," he said, but the child was already studying the faces of others on the skywalk and paid no more attention to him.

CHAPTER NINE

Lunch had been interesting. Barbecue pork on bamboo skewers, a salad made of green papaya that managed to be both sour and spicy at the same time, glutinous rice, and mangoes. It was the first time Sam had tried them and he could have eaten ten. They were wonderful. As it was, he was thoroughly distended and had welcomed Mrs. Cole's suggestion that he lie down for a bit after lunch.

The room was wonderfully cool now. He had broken the rules and left the air conditioning on while he was out shopping. He wiggled his toes to let the air refresh each one. Like a fool he had worn his oxfords back to the guesthouse when he should have changed into the sandals right in the store. But the oxfords were part of him and the sandals were not. The sandals reminded him of the flip-flops he wore on the beach many years ago in Kelowna when he, Alice, and the kids were on vacation. He hated the beach—one giant human barbecue—and he hated the lake, all full of kid pee. But sometimes he and Jeff would go fishing, pulling in those little sunfish and just throwing them back. Then one day Jeff started worrying about all these little fish swimming around with sore mouths and stopped doing it. After that they played miniature golf.

The memory was interrupted by a knock at the door.

"Come in."

Haddon poked his nose around the door and then entered. "Ah, now I know why you're in here," he said.

"I've already had enough sun to do me for the rest of my visit," Sam said.

Haddon laughed. "That was only morning sun. Wait until you experience afternoon sun." He sat down on the chair in the corner of the room. "So what did you do?"

Sam shrugged. "Bought some sandals."

"You're pretty brave going out there by yourself on the first day."

"Is it dangerous?"

"Not very, but it is alien, especially if it's your first time in Asia. May I see the sandals?"

Sam pointed to a plastic bag near Haddon's feet. Haddon opened the bag and extracted a pair of brown vinyl slip-on sandals. He inspected them carefully, checking the stitching and the tread. "How much did you pay?"

"Two hundred *baht*."

Haddon smiled and put the sandals back in the bag. "They'll do you for a while."

"Did I pay too much?" Sam asked.

"They'd have cost you more than that in Canada."

"But less than that here, right?"

"I paid ninety-five for a similar pair last week."

"Oh."

"Look at it this way. You paid less than you would have back home and you made somebody's day."

"I suppose," Sam said, grimacing.

"Anyway, we have a few details to iron out about your stay here. First of all, the cost of your stay is covered as far as we're concerned. You can stay in any of the mission's facilities for as long as you like, providing you give us some kind of time frame so we can make sure we have the space."

Sam shook his head. “No, I'll pay my own way. You guys aren't particularly well fixed. I can see that.”

“The mission still has money coming in for Jeff's support. I guess some people still think we have expenses connected to him. Anyway, the money to keep you is there and I'm sure Jeff's supporters wouldn't have any trouble with it being used in this way.”

Sam stood up and walked to the window and to the view of the courtyard beyond it. “Did he stay here often?”

“Whenever he was in Bangkok.”

“Was that often?”

“No, not really. But when he came, he stayed in this room.”

Sam looked back into the room and then at Haddon. “When can I see where you've put him?”

“We can go tomorrow if you like.”

* * *

The refrigerator in her father's home contained cold filtered water, Pepsi, and Singha beer. Chiang poured herself a glass of Pepsi and then added ice from the freezing compartment. She would have preferred the Singha but Lup Law had made it clear, after one indiscretion on her part, that the beer was intended solely for clients.

The clients were her father's well-heeled friends in town, occasional visitors from the provincial capital of Lopburi, or even important dignitaries from Bangkok. Such visitors were increasingly frequent in the house as her father's status increased. It was only a matter of time before the captain moved on to take charge of the police detachment in a much larger centre, a provincial capital, or even in Bangkok itself. But for now her father was focused on one thing, finding Ute.

Chiang carried the Pepsi across the large open room that made up most of the main floor and sat down on a rattan chair near the front of the house. A sliding large mesh metal door stood between her and the street. Outside this, alone on the sidewalk, her son was playing with his latest toy, a stuffed animal half way between a bear and a dog in appearance. This he kicked and threw around in a small child's imitation of *Muay Thai*, the national sport of Thailand.

Lup Law had a collection of fight videos that he liked to watch when he was drinking—something that was happening with increasing frequency as his problems finding Ute dragged on. When he watched, the child was often in the room. The first time the captain saw his grandson involved in this new form of play, he collapsed in laughter and gave the child candy. So now it was Wanlop's favourite form of play and his grandfather brought home a new opponent every two or three days. They didn't last long.

Chiang heard the approach of her father's BMW and put the Pepsi down. She went to the front of the house and slid open the metal door. The BMW drove in. Lup Law got out of the car and Wanlop ran toward him. One look from the captain stopped the boy dead in his tracks. He quickly ran over and grabbed his mother's leg.

"No, it wasn't the bike." Lup Law said, answering the unspoken question. He walked over to the refrigerator, opened the door, took out a Singha, looked at it blankly for a few moments, put it back, and then went to the cabinet were he kept his collection of imported spirits. Almost any bottle in the collection was worth half a month's wages for the average Thai. Having them was almost as important as having the BMW. He poured himself a shot from a bottle of Irish whiskey, drank it, and looked at his daughter.

"I can't understand, considering the way he treated you, why you're protecting him."

Chiang pulled Wanlop onto her lap. "I don't know where he is," she said. She wanted to add that she knew Ute did not kill Jep, but to argue so was pointless. Her father would launch into another long tirade about knowing all about her sleeping with Jep. They both knew this was a lie, but Lup Law had made it the basis of his excuse to implicate Ute and had to keep up the pretense even in front of his daughter.

"I'll get him. You know I will."

Chiang said nothing as her father poured himself another drink and headed for the video player.

* * *

Sam wished that Haddon had not mentioned that he was in Jeff's favorite room. It haunted the place and wouldn't let him sleep. He watched the *cheechaks*, read an Asian edition of *Time* magazine, and remembered things. Curiously most of them were not real memories at all but rather imaginings, images his mind had created while reading Jeff's letters and then stored as if they were real memories. They were both consistent and at odds with the reality of this place, the images were at odds and the feel was consistent. He took a shower in the middle of the night and then went outside to smoke until the mosquitoes drove him back inside. He fell asleep about dawn only to be woken by Haddon an hour later.

"We want to be on the road before the city gets moving," he said. "I've taken the liberty of buying some pastries for the journey."

Sam nodded, dressed quickly, stashed the luggage in one of the closets—in case the room was needed while he was gone—and grabbed the overnight bag he had packed at three a.m. He did his best to stay awake during the drive through the city, but by the outskirts he was out.

Sam's ears woke before his eyes. He found himself listening to the sounds of Haddon's pickup, the dry rasp of the air conditioner under the hum of the Japanese engine, and a tape of a well-trained male voice singing hymns to department-store orchestration barely louder than the automotive white noise. He tried to hear things outside the truck, but apart from the occasional whoosh of a passing vehicle, he heard nothing.

He had been fully awake now for at least five minutes, but somehow it became important to open his eyes as if he were just waking. He yawned first, stretched, and then allowed his eyelids to flicker open.

"Good morning," Haddon said.

"Is it still?"

"Yes, you slept for nearly two hours but it's still morning. Will be for another hour or so."

The view outside the window was of largely flat terrain. Most of this was covered with what looked like green and brown stubble or flattened grain. This was frequently punctuated by clumps of trees or an occasional outcropping of rock. Houses, mostly wooden and on stilts, hid in the trees. The trees themselves were a combination of palms and hardwoods. Other houses, these ones newer and made from cement or brick, stood closer to the road and lacked the surrounding vegetation of their wooden counterparts.

It was a rural area, that was clear, but there were still people everywhere. They sold things by the side of the road, herded the white, leathered, skinny cattle, and worked in the fields swathing the few remaining stands of rice with sickles. Mostly though, they just sat around in the shade.

"Where are we?" Sam asked.

"About ten minutes out of Lopburi city, the capital of the province."

"Where Jeff worked."

Haddon nodded. "The grave is in a village near the town of Khoksamrong, about forty-five minutes the other side of Lopburi."

Sam said nothing. Outside the pickup, things where beginning to look like outskirts, a few shops, larger houses, more trees and people. "How big a town is this?"

"I don't know, thirty-five, forty thousand, I guess."

"Not too big."

"Except for Bangkok, there really aren't any big cities in Thailand. Chiang Mai might be as high as 250,000 by now, but most of the provincial capitals are around this size. It's still a largely agrarian society."

"A lot of soldiers."

"Soldiers?"

"A lot of soldiers here," Sam said gesturing at the large numbers of uniformed people on the street.

"Oh, that." Haddon smiled. "Yes, it's a military town.

Quite a few bases here. They even run the local zoo."

"The military?"

Haddon nodded. "It's probably some kind of PR thing. They're the real power in this country. They like to do things periodically to enhance their public image." He turned off the highway onto a road leading into the town. "You'll have a chance to see some old ruins and stuff as we're driving through town. You might find that interesting."

"Cambodian?" Sam asked.

Haddon looked surprised. "Yes, that's right, although I think they actually prefer the term *Khmer*."

Sam nodded. "I read over Jeff's letters a few times before I came out. I remember him talking about that."

"There are some *Khmer* ruins here from about a thousand years ago and some Hindu things that even pre-date that, I think. This was also the place where one of the Thai kings from the last dynasty, I can't remember which one, first met the French ambassador. So you get a lot of French tourists here. Most of the ruins are related to Thai royalty, and they have a reasonable museum as well. And a world-famous monkey temple if you're into that sort of thing. Lopburi town has quite a bit to offer tourists actually, except facilities. Until recently there wasn't a decent hotel in the whole town."

Sam said nothing. The people on the street seemed to be moving in slow motion, going about their business lethargically.

Haddon gestured to their right. Behind a tall barbed wire fence Sam a saw a long, narrow, grassy mound about seventy-five meters in length. Bricks, reddish and chipped, lay strewn along the top, some in piles and others lying loose.

"That's the wall of some fortress, maybe a thousand years old," Haddon explained. "The archaeologists haven't got at it yet, so it's still in its virgin state. They won't let the tourists near it. They're afraid they'll dig up some priceless artifact or something. I guess previously a lot of stuff was spirited out of the country before the authorities realized what it was."

Sam looked at the mound again. "Looks like a giant grave. I'll tell you what they're going to find there. They're going to find a lot of stuff that was left behind by the dead. Stuff that was left behind by people who lived their lives thinking that they were doing something meaningful, maybe even important. People who were forgotten centuries ago."

Haddon pursed his lips but said nothing. The truck passed a pedicab piloted by a thin old man whose muscles strained beneath his loose and wrinkled skin. His mouth was open as he breathed and his teeth looked like Stonehenge. Behind him sat a fat woman wrapped in fine colored cloth. From one of her dusty feet dangled a broken rubber thong.

"How old is he?" Sam said gesturing at the pedicab driver.

Haddon looked in the rear-view mirror. "Not as old as he looks, I think. Probably about the same age as you."

"No retirement for him, I suppose."

Haddon shook his head, but Sam was looking out the window. Before him were the three ancient *Khmer* towers he had seen on the back of one of the Thai bank notes. A few tourists were taking pictures. Sam waited for an explanation from Haddon but none was forthcoming. Once bitten, he thought, and reached for one of the pastries on the seat beside him.

The town of Khoksamrong was smaller than Lopburi and had none of the provincial capital's redeeming features. There were no big white gleaming government buildings, no ancient ruins or museums, no new hotels or train stations, and no semblance of military order. There was dust, dust on old temples, in the streets full of shop houses, in the open-air market, in the orange crush buses, in the pedicabs and pickups, on the motorcycles and farm vehicles, and on the feet of the children who were leading a water buffalo down the rutted dirt road where Haddon was now driving the pickup.

"Our policy," Haddon said, "is to discourage any kind of financial dependence on us or on the Western church. We're not interested in planting churches full of rice Christians. We don't want them joining up just to get the perks. That not only makes for suspect spirituality but it means that the church will collapse if the missionaries are forced to leave. And that happens a lot in this part of the world."

Sam was only half-listening. Before him, in panoramic vision, was a world he had only seen before in small projected rectangles on Western living room walls. Homes made of discarded wood, metal, and plastic rested on stilts. They appeared ready to fall. Dirty children with open sores and clothed in rags, played games with old bits of wood and plastic bottles. Solitary men wore their cigarettes with the same resignation that they wore their faded T-shirts, shorts, and rubber sandals. Women, sitting together on straw mats beneath the houses, prepared food to the sound of Thai pop songs coming from small radios. They had animals too, dogs trying to steal the food, chickens pecking at anything, and pigs wallowing in black mud within inches of the women's mats.

"So we encourage them to be financially independent of us as much as possible. They pay for their own church buildings and build them on their own land wherever they can afford it. And this," Haddon said as he steered the truck around a curve in the road, "is where they can afford it."

A wide inverted V-shaped metal roof on narrow cement pillars gave shade to a green cement floor. The only wall was pale yellow and at the far end. On it was a simple cross. A pair of hands appeared to be holding it up. About a dozen makeshift benches of various sizes were arranged in sloppy rows near a small white pulpit in the front of the church, but most of the space was empty.

"No walls," Sam said.

Haddon parked the truck near the church. "It doesn't give much protection from the elements. That's true. But, on the other hand, it's cool and heat is the major element here, especially at this time of the year."

Beyond the church stood a simple but solidly constructed house. Its design was similar to the other houses in the village but the building materials had been purchased, not salvaged. The space beneath the house was cement rather than dirt and mud.

"And this is where Jeff is buried?" Sam asked as the two men got out of the truck.

Haddon gestured to a spot about a hundred meters beyond the church. "At the other end of the field out there they have a few plots. They couldn't put them too close to the village because some of the local people are afraid of spirits. The Thais cremate their dead."

As Haddon spoke, a small, slight, balding Thai man appeared beneath the house and began walking rapidly but awkwardly toward them. He wore unlaced heavy black boots that looked as if they were military issue. When he reached the two men he bowed to both Haddon and Sam but not in the self-depreciating manner of the woman at the guesthouse. Then he spoke to Haddon in Thai. Haddon nodded and then the man turned to Sam.

"Welcome, Jep's father," he said slowly. "I am Pastor Sanit."

"Thank you. You speak English?" Sam asked.

"A little, but *Adjan* Stuart will speak for me mostly." He turned and spoke rapidly in Thai to Haddon.

"He said he will give us something to drink first and then take us to see the grave."

Sam nodded and then the two men followed Sanit to the space under his house. Here there were a half-dozen folding chairs and a small table. On this sat a blue plastic thermal pot and an assortment of tumblers.

As Sam and Haddon sat down Sanit removed the lid to the pot and began ladling water into the tumblers. The pot contained a large floating chunk of ice and flower petals of some sort. Sanit passed a tumbler to Sam and watched as Sam cautiously lifted the glass to his mouth. Sam could smell the flowers but he wasn't sure he wanted to taste them. Sanit watched as Sam drank the first glass, smiled, refilled it for him, and then sat down beside them. As he did so, a rotund woman in wine stretch pants and a brownish floral blouse appeared, descending the stairs from the house above. She carried a tray with two small baskets made from leaves that were pinned together with what looked like toothpicks. She set these in front of the three men, smiled, bowed to Sam and Haddon, and went back up the stairs.

"My wife, Suk" Sanit said.

The baskets were full of white gelatinous circular-shaped objects that reminded Sam of the tops of mushrooms. They were specked with green and smelled of coconut.

"A local dessert," said Haddon. "Try one."

Sam studied the baskets for a moment and then shook his head. His eyes strayed back to the field beyond the house where Jeff was buried.

Haddon popped one of the sweets into his mouth and then stood up. "Yes, well, I guess we'd better do what we've come to do."

The three men walked out from under the house and in single file along an elevated path between two dry rice fields. There were four graves. Three of them were wind-worn mounds marked by simple crosses. The fourth was a fresher mound. On it was a metal marker with a hood to shade both Jeff's picture and the SOS logo.

"The only instructions that Jeff left us were that if something happened he wanted to be buried near the church where he was serving. He said nothing about a monument, so we thought we'd leave that up to you." Haddon turned and looked at Sam.

Sam said nothing. The photo affixed to the metal marker was already fading and the shape of the grave was much like that of the narrow grassy mounds of the archeological site they had seen earlier in Lopburi. Grass was growing on it. Sam reached out to touch the photo but stopped about three inches from it. He made a second attempt but this time his hand started to shake, so much so that he had to steady it with his other hand. There was a long pause.

"This won't be here," he said.

Haddon looked at him but said nothing.

"The picture will fade and fall apart and blow away. The metal will rust and dissolve. Maybe there will be a red stain on the ground where it used to be." Tears streamed down both of Sam's cheeks.

"I...I wonder what they'll say when they dig it up a thousand years from now," he said. "I...I wonder what meaning they'll give to it." He turned and began walking back along the narrow path between the rice fields.

CHAPTER TEN

The day of Sam's arrival in Khoksamrong became evening in a slow and leisurely fashion. Suk served a meal of barbecued chicken, rice, bamboo shoots, and a sweet coconut and banana dessert. Haddon and Sanit tried to engage Sam in conversation but he answered in monosyllables, and soon they began talking together in Thai. Sam watched them for a while, marveling at the ease of their friendship and wondering about Sanit's heavy black boots. Then he got up and walked slowly over to the back of the church, where he sat down on one of the benches with his back to the pulpit.

The people of the village were watching him. Their faces appeared between the boards of their houses. They gathered in small groups on the road and gestured in his direction. One man even rode his bicycle right up to the church, appraised Sam with interest, smiled, waved, and then rode back. His friends all laughed.

A pedicab rounded the turn driven by a man who might have been one of them. He wore a white canvas fisherman's hat, a T-shirt advertising Miller's brew, denim shorts, and canvas shoes that were ripped and torn nearly to the point of disintegration.

He had two passengers: a stocky muscular man with a wide jaw and high cheek bones, and a smaller older man with few teeth and a nose that was receding into his face. The older man had a crutch and a large plaster cast on one foot, while the other foot was turned in and missing several toes. Both carried black books. They got out of the pedicab, paid the driver, gave him a tract, and began walking slowly toward Sanit's house.

A few minutes later a man and a woman on a motorcycle arrived. They parked the bike under Sanit's house and began greeting the people who were already there. Then a young man on a bicycle and two more women in another pedicab arrived. These two gave Sam a cheery wave, being the first to notice him sitting motionless in the back of the church. They pointed him out as they greeted the others, but Haddon shook his head in what Sam assumed was an instruction to leave him alone. He got up and walked back to the house.

"What's going on?" Sam asked after bowing to several people.

"Sorry, I forgot this is their night for a dusk-to-dawn prayer meeting," Haddon said. "I'm afraid we won't get much sleep tonight. At least I won't. Part of my ministry, you understand. I'm sure they'll find a quiet corner for you. Of course you're welcome to come along, if you like. You'll be the subject of much prayer, in any case."

As they spoke, another couple arrived on a motorcycle; a young man and a much older woman. This time it was the woman who had obvious physical difficulties. Her left hand was curled inward and she wore large wide sandals for her crippled feet. Her blotched skin stretched tightly over her face and there was no evidence of cartilage in either her nose or her ears. The young man parked the motorcycle and helped her off. He then got back on the bike and drove off quickly.

A radiant smile spread over the woman's face as she approached the group and greeted each of the others with great enthusiasm. When she got to Sam, she stopped and looked at him questioningly for a moment. Then, as Sam watched, a tear formed in one of her eyes and then slid over the blotched skin to a spot just above her mouth. She made no attempt to wipe it off.

"*Dichan rak khun Jep,*" she said.

Sam looked at Haddon for the translation.

"She said she loved your son. Her name is Mrs. Boon-Mi. She's one of the few Christians living in Banmi. She's been ill much of the past few years and Jeff has been a great help. He ran a lot of errands for her and even took her to the Christian hospital in Singburi. He took care of her while she was there. No one in her family was willing to go."

"Took care of her?"

"Out here the hospitals only look after your medical needs. This means you have to take a relative or friend along to look after your food, laundry, toiletries—that kind of thing. Usually they stay right there in the hospital with the patient, sleeping on the floor beside the bed."

"Jeff did that?"

"Well, I imagine he slept at the missionary guesthouse while at the hospital, but he did all the rest of it, yes. It was quite a witness, actually, spoke volumes to the people in town. It also embarrassed the family rather badly. They've been quite conscientious about meeting her needs ever since. That was her nephew who brought her here tonight."

"So what happens now?"

Haddon looked at his watch and grinned sheepishly. "Well, in about ten minutes everyone will go upstairs, sit on the floor, and watch TV."

"TV?"

"The news, actually. And if there's anything on that needs to be prayed about, they'll do it during the meeting. That's the theory anyway." Haddon shrugged. "Sanit is the only person in the church who owns a TV. A retiring missionary gave it to him. He feels he has to share it."

"Oh."

Sanit came over and spoke to Haddon and then they both went over to talk with someone who had just arrived. Sam stood up and walked out from underneath the house. It was now nearly dark, but the pathway to the graves was still clearly visible. He found himself standing before Jeff's grave trying in vain to make out the image that had been posted there.

Mosquitoes were biting. He looked back at the house and saw that everyone had gone inside. He turned and looked at the grave again. The metal marker now looked like a shovel that had been stuck upside down in the dirt. He walked back to the house and climbed the stairs.

The people, a group now numbering about sixteen, were seated on the floor in front of a fourteen-inch television, watching a talking head. Their backs were to Sam as he entered the room. A few acknowledged his arrival by turning and nodding their heads, but most never let their gaze stray from the set. Sam found a piece of floor large enough to accommodate him and carefully lowered himself into a cross-legged sitting position similar to the men. He was able to hold this for about forty seconds, after which he knew that he would need considerably more leg room and something with which to prop up his back.

Haddon, who was sitting close by, leaned over to him.

"I wouldn't even try to sit like that if you're not used to it. Especially at your age. It will give you a terrible cramp." Haddon was sitting like that, but he changed his position to one where both legs where bent at the knee but going in the same direction. "Try this. It's how the women sit here, but they expect it of foreign men."

Sam looked around the room to catch the group's reaction to Haddon's new posture. No one seemed bothered by it, so he allowed himself to change. Relief was immediate, but the floor was still hard.

A pillow thudded into his lap. "*Kha thod, na kha,*" said a woman across the room from him. She smiled as he slid the pillow beneath him.

* * *

Lup Law had annexed the street in front of his house. At one end, a large portable movie screen had been erected and, at the other, a bandstand. In between they had set up a tent covering twenty round tables with six to eight chairs each. Inside the invited guests were eating seafood from the coast, pork, chicken, imported beef, rice and vegetables.

Liquor, both domestic and imported, was everywhere. Chiang smiled grimly. Ever since she was a small child she had wondered about these parties. They were thrown to celebrate the initiation of a young man into the holy Buddhist monkhood, but during the party any number of the Buddhist prohibitions were broken. Animals had to be killed for the meat, alcohol was consumed, people went off to secret or not-so-secret sexual liaisons. There were loud arguments or even fights fueled by the drink. The men were often found gambling in a corner. There was nothing holy in any of this as far as she could tell.

Tanait agreed. Though he was present at the festivities he did not get involved in the revelries, confining himself to a table under one of the tents. From here he greeted people, accepted their well wishes and thanked them for coming.

Chiang nodded in the direction of her mother and sister and stood up from the table. The noise from the band made normal conversation impossible, and Wanlop had wandered off and was now dancing with his latest stuffed victim in front of the bandstand. The boy was far too close to the PA system and Chiang feared for his hearing. She grabbed him and carried the struggling child back to the table where her mother and sister were sitting. A group of family friends had stopped to congratulate her mother on Tanait's initiation.

"Look at him," a lady said to her, pointing at Tanait. "You'd think he was already a monk. Lucky woman, he will bring you much good karma."

Dokmai smiled and thanked them but when they had left she looked over at her son who sat passively watching the action in front of him. "You might as well get up and enjoy yourself," she shouted to him. "It will be your last chance for a while."

"It's enough that everyone else is enjoying themselves."

"Suit yourself." Then she smiled as another group of family friends approached. This group was a Chinese family. They owned the two largest sapphire-polishing sweatshops in town.

The patriarch of the group was plump, balding and paling into yellow. He spent his time ensconced behind a desk in his air-conditioned office in back of the larger of his two shops. There he burned incense to the multiple gods on his Buddha shelf, bribed officials including Chiang's father, planned the future of his two sons and, of course, made money. Lots of money. That was his routine. In the last few years, however, he'd also developed an obsession. He spent hours each day poring over the catalogues from monument companies, trying to decide how to best immortalize himself when his time came.

Chiang knew all of this because the eldest son, Samyong, had taken more than a passing interest in her in the days before Ute. They had discussed their families numerous times over Pepsis in the open-air restaurants during the hot season. It was the only time of year when Samyong was at home from the exclusive school he attended in Bangkok. They had even discussed marriage, planning to elope if Samyong was forced to marry the Chinese girl from Bangkok to whom he had already been promised.

She was now there at his side, a tiny wisp of a thing with no hips to bear children. They had been married two years earlier, shortly after the robust Samyong had mysteriously failed the army draft medical exam, something rich Chinese boys did with bewildering regularity. Now Samyong ran the smaller of the two sweat shops and his wife stayed in the house the old man had built them, did her face, and pined for Bangkok.

Samyong's eyes had not met Chiang's since her pregnancy became common knowledge. Now that she was back to looking good again, thanks to her father's food, they roamed all over her body. Samyong's eyes took it all in. He smiled awkwardly at her, and she could feel his longing. She picked up the squirming Wanlop, pulled him onto her lap and returned Samyong's smile. He turned away quickly and obviously. His wife shot him a puzzled glance.

Lup Law chose that moment to return from greeting other guests. He exchanged bows with the old man and inquired about his business.

"I've had much good luck. Things are back to normal after the trouble." The old man paused for a moment and studied Lup Law. Chiang could tell they shared some secret knowledge. "Now what about you?" the old man said. "How is your police work going these days?"

"Every day we make progress," Lup Law said.

The old man's face hardened momentarily, then he forced a smile and nodded. He and his family moved off to occupy a nearby table.

Chiang looked at her father. She could tell the exchange with the elderly Chinese man had caused him to lose face. What did Samyong's father have on him? Wanlop squirmed in her lap and she let him down.

Images began to flicker on the screen at the other end of the street. Her father had chosen an American movie, *Romancing the Stone*, to be the first film after Tanait had shown no interest in the subject. "Lots of action and a beautiful woman," he'd said. And cartoon voices, Chiang added mentally. She could never figure out why the Thai film distributors always used cartoon voices to dub foreign films. She preferred Thai films. At least the voices were normal and moved with the lips.

Chiang turned and looked at her sister. Wanlop had gone over to Lek and was now in the process of nodding off in her lap. Chiang did not feel slighted, but rather relieved. Her son and her sister had developed a special bond. "Do you love him?" Chiang asked her, but the sound of the movie drowned out the question. It was an unnecessary question in any case. She watched her sister cradle the boy and then looked back at her mother. Dokmai's eyes were unfocused, internal. Chiang took one last look at her brother sitting passively at his table. "I hope you find what you're looking for," she said but again she was not heard. She stood up and walked to the house. She would not look again for Lup Law. She preferred to remember him losing face in front of Samyong's father.

Chiang collected the bag she had prepared and then walked out the back door, through the trees and along the railway tracks to the station. In three hours she would be in Bangkok. Her father would lose his hoard of American money and two of his children that day, though it might be awhile before he understood about Tanait.

* * *

They prayed and they sang. They read from their Bibles, ate guavas and oranges, and laid their hands upon one another, sometimes with tears. Sam watched, drank the flower water, and thought long and deep about Jeff, wondering how his son had behaved among these people.

About midnight Sanit turned to Sam. "And now we must know how we should pray for you, Jep's father," he said in English.

"Pray for me?"

"Yes, how should we pray?"

Sam looked at Haddon, who nodded. He turned back to Sanit. "You can pray that I find the man who killed my son."

Sanit looked to Haddon for a moment but Haddon said nothing. The pastor turned to the others and spoke to them. Several of them came over, laid their hands on Sam, and began to pray.

* * *

Larry shuffled slowly down the hallway and turned into his room, all without touching a wall or doorframe. He walked seven paces into the room, made a ninety-degree turn clockwise and then slowly lowered himself into a cross-legged sitting position before three large cardboard boxes. He reached slowly into the box closest to the door and lightly touched a cassette tape within. He smiled.

"Amy Grant, *Unguarded*," he said softly in English. The house was finally becoming his. Barring unforeseen obstacles, he could now move anywhere within it without help and without touching walls. He also had his cassettes back the way they had been before the move. It was now easy to find the one he wanted without having to run his fingers over every one.

Larry took the cassette, stood up and slowly walked over to a table in the corner of the room. On it was a Sony tape machine, a gift from a missionary friend. He momentarily turned the radio on. "BBC World Service," a horticulture program. He turned it off. The BBC was one of the English-language stations he listened to regularly. This was the reason his English was as good as it was, but he wasn't interested in plants. He put the cassette in the machine and turned it on.

The song *Love of Another Kind* blasted forth and Larry began mentally naming each chord as it came along. He had taken two years of music lessons at the Catholic school for the blind, but he had no instrument on which to practice. He did, however, have perfect pitch and he had learned to identify any chord, even those with strange intervals, after hearing them only once. Even a rapid passing chord. Larry harbored a fantasy that some day he would be discovered by an orchestra leader, preferably a jazz musician, who would use his skill to chart obscure jazz tunes directly off the record. His head swayed gently and the fingers of his right hand moved as if playing an imaginary keyboard. Amy Grant was not jazz but she was gospel, the next best thing.

The music was loud, loud enough to drown out the approaching footsteps of his mother. Her light touch on his shoulder startled him.

"Larry, there's someone on the phone for you," she said. "A foreigner," she added. She did not like missionaries. It was a missionary who'd began calling her son Larry rather than his Thai name Nung. Her son now preferred the English name.

"Thank you," he said. He got up and followed her to the phone, touching the walls as he did so because he wanted to move quickly. It had been several weeks since the last time he'd heard from one of his missionary friends.

"Larry, how would you like to earn some money?"

"Hello, Stuart," Larry replied. Stuart always started conversations in the middle without greeting him first. "How are you? I haven't heard from you in a long time."

"I'm fine but I've been pretty busy. You know about Jeff Watson, of course."

Larry had met with Jeff while the young missionary was studying Thai in Bangkok. He had come to Larry a few times to get help with his Thai, but the relationship hadn't lasted, largely because of the distance Jeff was forced to travel. The language study centre and Larry's old house were on opposite sides of Bangkok. Jeff had given him a number of cassettes as a thank-you gift, some jazz and a lot of contemporary gospel. Then he went up-country to work and they lost contact.

"I heard that someone murdered him a couple of months back. They told me at church. I was upset, of course, but whenever I tried to reach you, the line was busy."

"I'm sorry, Larry. I should have called you and filled you in, but there was so much to deal with that calling you didn't even cross my mind. It's been hard on us all."

There was a pause. Larry had heard the fatigue in Stuart's voice. He almost didn't want to ask the question but felt he had to. "I've heard the radio reports, of course, but haven't had a chance to talk to anyone from the mission. How did it happen?"

Stuart told the story of Jeff's death and all the difficulties connected to it. Larry listened in silence, trying to figure out what they might have for him in this, but nothing was obvious. "Stuart, I don't think I understand how I can help you," he finally said.

"Well, Larry, the thing is we have a small problem on our hands. Jeff's death brought us a lot of attention we didn't want, a lot of unfair negative publicity in the local press. Rumors of Jeff's involvement with the Banmi police captain's married daughter and other things of that nature have led to a lot of missionary bashing in the papers. It's all pretty much gone by now, of course, but part of the reason for that is our refusal to cooperate with the investigation or to respond to the criticisms. We've been very quiet, so the press has lost interest. Initially we got Jeff's family, which is really just his father, to agree to this. That was not an easy thing to do, because until quite recently Jeff's father was an officer with the Vancouver city police in Canada. He's a man who believes in justice, in law and order. He's not a Christian, so our concern with preserving the missionary presence here isn't having much of an impact. I don't think he's that fond of us, maybe because he was against his son coming out here in the first place. I don't know.

Anyway, he arrived in Thailand about a week ago and he wants to pursue the investigation of Jeff's death by himself. He says he understands our position, so he wants to do it independently. It's his right, I guess. We've been taking him around for the past few days, showing him the sights, talking to him about the country, explaining our work, taking him out to the grave site, that kind of thing. But we really can't be involved with what he wants to do and that means he'll need an interpreter."

Larry laughed. "The blind leading the deaf."

"What do you think?"

Larry did not immediately answer. "You know what I've been doing these past few months?"

"No, what?"

"Learning to move around this house without touching the walls. I can do it. As long as no one puts things in my way and I take it slow, I can do it." He paused.

"Feeling secure there, are you?"
"Yes, but also bored."
"It will be hard."
"Can I meet him before I say?"
"Yes, of course."
"Does he know I'm blind?" Larry asked
"No."
"Remind him that he is deaf."

CHAPTER ELEVEN

Eating had always been Ouan's way of dealing with anything that bothered him. Minor problems were met with ice cream, fried bananas, or shrimp chips; major ones with full meals at odd times of the day, and crises with continuous intoxicating binges. Twice in the past week someone had asked about the motorcycle under the sheet in front of his home. On both occasions the persons had been unknown to him. Now he ate continuously, stopping only to go and find another restaurant when the owners of the current one began to show discomfort at his constant presence. He was running out of money and had not been home for several days. His instincts told him to run, to get out of town, but he was not a runner. He was an eater. Somehow being bloated carried with it the illusion of security.

Seated across from him in the restaurant were three men, an elderly Chinese fellow and two young, fit, and intense Thais. Was it his imagination or were they watching him? He had been nursing a large plate of rice and curry, eating just fast enough to maintain a continuous feeling of fullness. Now he sped up. It was unnecessary. He had already paid for the meal. He could get up and walk out without arousing suspicion. But he had to eat it. He wolfed it down, attracting the men's attention as he did so. He stood up and began walking toward the door.

"Friend," said the Chinese man. "Come and sit with

us."

Ouan turned and looked at the man. He was well dressed and wore a huge diamond ring on the middle finger of his left hand. He smiled and beckoned to Ouan. His two companions made no such pretense. To them Ouan was the quarry. He was both too fat and too full to run. They knew it and he knew it. He walked over, bowed with maximum respect, and sat down in the chair provided.

"First, I should introduce myself," said the Chinese man. "My name is Somsak and I am a financier from Nakhon Sawan."

A loan shark, thought Ouan. He raced through his memories trying to remember if anyone might be after him for a bad loan. The only thing that came to mind was Ute's bike.

"A while back a young police officer came to me and borrowed money to buy a motorcycle, a very expensive motorcycle. I loaned it to him because he seemed to be well connected and, of course, being a police officer, he should have been able to make the payments. You can understand my dismay when both he and the motorcycle disappeared before a single payment was made. I have since learned that he was not a police officer, although he had been one in the past. He is also wanted for questioning with regard to the murder of that foreigner who was killed a few months back in Lopburi province." Somsak paused and leveled his gaze at Ouan. Ouan gave him a weak smile.

"We found the motorcycle yesterday under a sheet in front of your house. Your neighbours told us that it's been there for over three months and that you never ride it. I can only assume you're holding it for our ex-policeman friend. You realize that technically you're in possession of stolen property?"

The color drained from Ouan's face. "I, uh..."

Mr. Somsak cut him off with a wave of his hand. "I can get the police to do pretty much anything I want. I think you know that. But in this case I wanted to get the bike before they did because, with such a high profile case—they've even had foreign journalists looking into this—who knows how long the bike would have been in their custody before it would have been returned to me? I don't like having my property tied up like that. So I guess I have you to thank that I have the motorcycle back." He smiled. "No police officer would have ever thought to look in such an obvious place." He regarded Ouan seriously. "Since you have done me this favor, I will do one for you. Simply tell me where your ex-policeman friend is and I'll forget about the whole thing."

* * *

Pastor Sanit's house only had one actual bed, a single one at that. It sat in a corner of the house behind a movable screen and was used primarily by visiting missionaries. The bed sagged and gave off a slight odor of mildew, but this was not what kept Sam awake. Throughout the night his mind went continually to the prayers and singing of the unfortunate people on the other side of the screen. They prayed their individual prayers simultaneously, out loud, and often with great emotion. *God must be great to sort all that out*.

At least half of the people showed signs of leprosy. "They're all cured, but they still carry the scars," Haddon had explained. This didn't stop Sam from being concerned. A number of them had, after all, placed their hands on him when they prayed. Not that he was worrying about it at the time. He had allowed himself to experience the event without thinking about it too much, as if suspending cognitive functions would somehow allow him to understand the religious side of things. It hadn't worked. He felt strange standing in the middle of a bunch of people who were touching him and muttering over him in a language he didn't understand.

After it was over he was exhausted. Haddon noticed him drooping and told Sanit, who showed Sam to the bed. It was then that he noticed the pastor's feet, which were a twisted mess, and realized that Sanit, too, had the disease.

He kept telling himself that Jeff had worked among these people for eight years without contracting the it. Sam knew that leprosy was now easily cured and only a problem if not treated. Why, he asked himself, was he, a man who had spent his life facing far more dangerous situations, bothered by this? Was it really the leprosy that bothered him, or was it something else? If so, what? He had no answers, but his mind replayed the faces of the people in the village. Then, when he finally drifted off to sleep, their faces were replaced by the faces of those he'd known in Vancouver's inner city. In the dream he moved among them as a leper.

* * *

In the morning, the motorcycle that had stood outside of Ouan's house was gone. In its place was Ouan's body wrapped in the sheet.

* * *

As a precaution, Chiang got off the train at the Don Muang station. She thought it unlikely that her father had yet sounded the alarm. He was probably much too busy with Tanait's party to spend much time wondering about her absence. Still there was a chance. If he had sounded the alarm, there was little doubt he would know that she was on the train—several people had seen her at the station in Banmi—and if he knew she was on the train, then it was almost certain someone would be watching the passengers get off at Bangkok's main terminal. She'd bought a ticket to the main terminal knowing her father would find out. The Don Muang station, located right across from the airport and several stops before the main terminal, was the last place that would be watched. Only a handful of people from Banmi had ever been overseas. They were either rich or had gone to Saudi Arabia as contract laborers. She was neither. Her father would not expect her to go the airport.

It was past midnight and several hours before buses would start taking people into the city again. Taxis were available, but they were expensive. She would wait in the airport until morning.

* * *

Despite a virtually sleepless night, Haddon was up early. He had business at the hospital in Singburi, but said he would give Sam a quick tour of Banmi before going.

"It'll just be a drive-through, you understand. Philip is

showing a young American doctor around the hospital in hopes that he may be the answer to our need for a surgeon. He's inexperienced and a recent believer, but his parents are Thais living in Los Angeles so he may be able to get around the visa restrictions. With Philip about to retire, we'll need someone quick if we're going to keep the place open." Haddon gave Sam a pat on the knee as he drove the truck away from the church. "Don't worry, as soon as we find a decent interpreter for you, you can spend as much time in Banmi as you want."

Sam nodded. "You sure you'll be all right to drive?"

"I'll be okay. I do this all the time. If I can get into Singburi by 9:30, I'll take one of the guest rooms and get a couple of hour's sleep before the meeting. On a decent bed, too." Haddon shook his head and smiled grimly. "Fourteen years in this country and I still can't sleep on a straw mat. Anyway, that will give you a chance to explore the place a bit. It's quite beautiful. One of Jeff's favorite spots, right on the river. He went there for a couple of days several times a year. He'd spend his mornings encouraging people on the wards, sharing his faith if they were open to it. Then he'd spend his afternoons and evenings praying as he watched the river."

The truck cleared the village and emerged on a paved road. Haddon turned right, and about two hundred meters later pulled up to an uncontrolled intersection. A small white shelter stood by the intersection. A policeman sat on a bench outside cleaning his gun.

Haddon gestured to him. "If you're a police officer in this country, you have to buy your own gun. By local standards that's a pretty hefty investment, so you tend to take good care of your weapon."

"What's he doing here? Traffic detail?"

"That's the official line, I'm sure. Maybe it's what he does most of the time, but I find the location of this particular police box interesting."

"Why's that?"

"See those buildings across the road over there?"

About fifty meters down the road and set back about thirty-five meters was a haphazard collection of buildings made of wood and corrugated metal. Two young women were sitting in the shade eating from bowls.

"What is it?"

"The local brothel."

"Is it legal?"

Haddon shook his head. "Prostitution is technically illegal in Thailand. But that place has been doing a roaring business ever since I've known about it. Get the picture?"

"Paid protection."

Haddon turned right and the town of Khoksamrong began receding behind them. "The thing is, in this part of the world, Mr. Watson, the police don't occupy the moral high ground. They make most of their money from corruption. We had a convert in the police academy in Saraburi a while back, a nice young man. He was active in the church and had a real hunger for the Word. Then he graduated and went to work. His duty sergeant kept telling him to take bribes from people and got very upset when he didn't. After a while, the man stopped coming to church. He'd found his own heaven in the form of a motorcycle, TV, VCR, nice clothes..."

"What kind of wages do the police get?"

"Subsistence, really. Probably works out to about a

thousand a year, American. You can survive on that, but you won't be buying a lot of extras. I haven't met a police officer yet who didn't live well above his means."

Sam shook his head. "I can't see how the people wouldn't have much respect for the system if that's how it works."

Haddon shrugged. "They haven't known any other. In this country, if you're in a position of power, you're expected to take money under the table. It's not only the police. It's the civil service, the military, government, business... That's just how things work here. If you have the power to get things done, you can expect to profit under the table."

"And what about him?" Sam said gesturing to a man herding cattle by the side of the road.

Haddon smiled. "He's learned to live with the system and he'll expect to profit by it if he ever gets into a position of power."

"So there's no right or wrong as far as the people are concerned?"

"No, I wouldn't say that. Most of them think the system is wrong. If you ask them, they'll tell you it's corrupt. They'll also tell you that, if you want to get ahead, you have to work within the system."

Sam looked at Haddon. "So what about your organization? What about the Siam Outreach Society? Does it play within the system?"

Haddon shook his head. "John the Baptist told the Roman soldiers not to take bribes, that they should be content with their pay. We don't believe Christians should participate in corruption."

"Then how do you get ahead?"

"By prayer and patience, mostly. But then the game

isn't quite the same for us as it is for the nationals. For example, a while back our house girl was trying to get her motorcycle driver's license. She's a Christian and had made a decision not to get involved with corruption. She was a good motorcyclist, but every time she took the examination they failed her. She wasn't putting money under the table. But when my son went in—he was barely able to handle a motorcycle at the time—they gave him the license for the standard fee without his even having to take the test. You see if *we* go in and play dumb they're not about to explain the corruption in the system. That would make them lose face. So, often they'll just give you what you want to get you out of the way. But the girl grew up here and so, of course, she's expected to know how things are done."

"Then you can get things done faster than a national can?"

"Well, not necessarily, and that's where the patience comes in. A motorcycle license is a pretty small item. Start asking for more work permits or permission to build a hospital and things get a lot slower. At that level there's a lot of people in the system with big money to throw around, and when they throw it they always wind up in front of you in the line. We can often wait years for permission to do some things."

"But, in the day to day things, you can get things done easier?"

"Well, that's often the case, yes." Haddon frowned.

Sam looked at him squarely. "You know I'm having a problem with this don't you?"

"How so?"

"Look, I have as much of a problem with corruption as the next guy. I spent a good portion of my life fighting it in one form or another. But it's also pretty obvious to me that you people have a lot more resources at your disposal than the people you're working with. I mean, I used to think Jeff was nuts taking the kind of wages he did to do this. But even that tiny stipend you gave him would have put his standard of living way beyond that of all these leprosy people. And then you got the gall to come in here and introduce them to a religion that's only going to make their lives more difficult. What you should be doing is trying to change the system, but what you're really doing is trying to change the heart of some poor guy, a guy who's totally powerless when it comes to changing the system. And when you succeed, you write these nice little letters home to your supporters telling them of Joe such and such's wonderful conversion. What you've really done is made his life nearly impossible to live."

Haddon said nothing.

"Well?" asked Sam.

Haddon spoke reluctantly. "What the Jews in first-century Palestine wanted Jesus to do was to liberate them from the Roman system. What He actually did was to talk to them about their relationship with God and ultimately give His life so that relationship could be renewed."

"So?"

"He didn't have many rich and influential followers; not many people who could have had much of an impact on the injustices of the day. And there were plenty of problems. But it wasn't until a few hundred years after his death and resurrection that the church actually started to gain some influence in those areas. The point is that improvements in justice—and 'the system' if you like—come after one is renewed in one's relationship with God."

From the look on Haddon's face, Sam could tell he wasn't expecting Sam to buy this argument. All the same, Haddon didn't look like someone who was just parroting the official line. He believed it. Sam decided to try another angle. "So what you're telling me is that you expect things to improve for these people in a couple of hundred years?"

"Sooner than that we hope."

Sam shook his head. "I don't know how much Jeff told you about our family."

"Not much. Just that his mother was dead and that you weren't all that crazy about him coming out here."

Sam pursed his lips. "My wife, Alice, was a fundamentalist Christian, a real Bible thumper. In the early years of our marriage we attended this big church. Well, she attended it more than I did. And this church had really good acoustics, a red carpet throughout, expensive grand piano, big organ with pipes growing out of the walls...everything was first class. And programs...It was programmed to the hilt. Youth groups, college and career, seniors clubs, Bible studies going on all the time, summer camps...I mean the thing was set up so that you could spend all of your non-working and non-sleeping time doing something at the church. And that's what a lot of the people did. They hung out at the church. It was the internal focus of the thing that got to me. I mean I was out there dealing with street kids, criminals, prostitutes, and various different kinds of injustice and my wife's church was organizing picnics. Why? To get people closer to God. But it's a god that's apparently not interested in the kinds of people I was dealing with. I can tell you that the amount of money set aside in that church budget to deal with social issues of any kind didn't amount to a hill of beans."

Haddon said nothing. He gestured to buildings that were beginning to appear by the side of the road and then to a bridge in front of them. "When we get over that bridge we'll be in Banmi," he said.

The bridge was new. Materials unused in its construction were still in piles on the side of the road. A purely functional cement arch, it spanned a muddy brown body of water that was perhaps seventy-five meters across and disappeared in straight lines in either direction. Beneath the bridge, several ark shaped wooden boats were secured. Two of these had laundry lines running the length of them and a third was serving as a diving ramp for young swimmers.

"It's a man made canal, built about twenty years ago for irrigation," Haddon said. "It took them this long to get a decent bridge built over it."

The outskirts of Banmi unfolded in much the same way as those of Khoksamrong. The buildings were primarily two-story shop houses, some older and wooden, some newer and cement. These were punctuated here and there by small institutional buildings like the post office. And, as in Khoksamrong, dust was everywhere. As they approached the town centre, however, Sam noticed a difference between the two towns. Although Banmi was smaller than Khoksamrong, the town centre was much newer and more affluent.

"There are two reasons for that," Haddon said responding to Sam's query. "The first is that there was a big fire about seven years back that destroyed much of the downtown core. It had to be rebuilt. The second is that the merchants have a lot more money here than they have in Khoksamrong. I'm sure Jeff told you about the gem-polishing industry."

"Yeah, he did. None too positively, I might add."

"Maybe, if I get more time, I'll take you in to visit a couple of the sweat shops."

He made a turn onto a side street and then brought the vehicle to an abrupt halt. Across the street a temporary barricade had been erected. Beyond this a group of workers were busy dismantling a stage and what looked like an outdoor restaurant.

"Looks like we had a little party here last night. Probably to celebrate a *buat phra* for the son of one of the rich merchants."

"A what?"

"A *buat phra*. Every Thai young man is expected to spend a few months being a Buddhist monk in order to earn good karma for his mother. Usually the night before the initiation there's a party. How big a party depends on how wealthy his parents are." Haddon gestured to the dismantling. "This fellow's parents are pretty well off."

"Oh."

"This street, by the way, is where Jeff lived during his first term here, when he was teamed up with John Wexler. The two of them shared one of the smaller shop front places near the end. They wanted to be in the market so they could make the Gospel more visible. But the place was hot and noisy, especially when all night parties like this were going on, so Jeff moved further out in his second term."

“They really put a lot of work into those things, don't they?” Sam said, referring to the large ornate Buddhist temple they were slowly driving past. The building and the others in the temple grounds stood out in stark contrast to the simple wooden houses around them.

“Most Thais think that the best way to acquire good karma is to build or contribute to the building of a temple. I’m not so sure that agrees with the real teachings of Buddhism but that’s the popular notion anyway. So the people in the surrounding area may be in great poverty, but the money will always be found to build a fancy temple. Of course, it's usually only the rich who can afford to acquire good karma in this way.”

Sam laughed. “Kind of reminds me of the legal system back home. If you can afford a really good lawyer you’ll get a more *just* outcome in court.”

“Yes, but out here being rich is seen as a sign that you’ve led a particularly holy past life. All the good that you did in your previous life results in rewards for you in your present life. It might be wealth, status, or good looks. It might even be such things as athletic ability or intelligence. But particularly with things like wealth and status it carries with it a certain sense of moral superiority. The higher you are in terms of status, the greater your spiritual status in past lives must have been. So if you happen to be the king, you're so good it's against the law for anyone to criticize you, no matter what you do. And that applies not only to the present king, but to all past kings. Thai history books, particularly those actually published in Thailand, read like the lives of great saints.”

“Really?”

“Out here, Mr. Watson, criticizing Thai royalty in

public can land you in prison."

Haddon piloted the pickup around a curve in the road, and then turned left down a lane. Where the lane ended were three houses. Two of these were traditional Thai wooden houses on stilts, large and in good repair. The third house was also large. It, however, rested on the ground, had a conventional Western-style door with a lock and multiple large windows with metal bars instead of glass panes. Haddon gestured to it.

"That's it," he said.

"A pretty big place for a single man."

Haddon nodded. "We thought so, too, but Jeff managed to rent it for half the price of the place in town. Can't argue with that. Plus it has lots of space for meetings."

"Do you still have possession of it?" Sam asked.

"We've renegotiated the lease so it runs out at the end of the month. Technically, it's still ours for the next two weeks. But there's nothing in there. Everything's been removed." Haddon pointed to a miniature temple like house that stood on a post at the edge of the property. A bottle of Coke, a tangerine, and a couple of burned sticks of incense stood in front of it. "The owners have already come around and put the spirit house back up. I suspect it's only the first of a series of things they'll do to cleanse the place for the next renters. The Thais are very superstitious about violent death."

"Can I take a look inside?" Sam asked.

Haddon turned off the truck's engine and climbed out. "There's not much to see. It's empty. The owner insisted that we remove everything related to Jeff. That was a condition to our being able to get out of the lease."

He walked over to the house, unlocked the door, and

stood aside while Sam entered. A thin layer of dust had settled on the hardwood floor, but someone had disturbed this recently.

"The landlord," Haddon said, anticipating Sam's question. "He has a key."

Sam walked slowly through the huge room that made up eighty-five percent of the floor space. There was nothing there he could connect to Jeff. But Jeff had lived there for the last three years of his life. Sam tried to imagine what the room would have looked like with Jeff in it. Would he have had a predominance of Thai things? Western things? Sam's memory of Jeff's last apartment in Vancouver was completely at odds with this place.

"Where did he sleep?" he asked.

"Right in the middle of the room beneath the ceiling fan," Haddon answered. "He had a folding mattress that he stored in the corner during the day."

Sam's eye detected movement and he looked up to see an old woman watching him from the house across the lane. "Not very private," he said.

Haddon shrugged. "They can see into your house and you can see into theirs. There are few secrets among neighbours here."

"Did he get along with them?"

"Oh, they loved him. His presence made them all celebrities in the local market. They had him over for meals, took him to cultural events, came over for English lessons...He gave them books, rides into town on his motorcycle...He knew almost everyone in the area by name."

"Yet someone obviously had it in for him."

Haddon nodded. "Come on, there's something else."

Sam followed as Haddon went out the door, past the pickup, and down a footpath between the two houses on the opposite side of the lane. As they walked down the path, the people in both houses watched them. Sam caught the gaze of one of them, a small elderly man who acknowledged Sam with a bow and a little wave. Sam returned the wave and the man looked pleased.

The path took them between two stands of trees and then to a road. The road bordered a field where workers were swathing rice by hand. Beside it was a stone over which hung two floral garlands. Haddon stopped here and the two men watched the workers in silence for a few moments.

"Apparently," said Haddon, "Jeff was just standing here watching workers transplant rice when someone pulled up behind him on a motorcycle and put two bullets into him."

Sam felt his face flush. He looked at Haddon. "Here?"

Haddon nodded and gestured to the workers. "They're harvesting what was planted that day."

> They were both standing on the crest of a hill in the ranch lands northeast of Calgary. Father and son, each had his hands thrust deep into the pockets of their lined jean jackets. Sam's rifle was pressed between his left arm and body, the barrel pointing into short brown grass at his feet. Sam felt the weight of it. There had been no deer that day, only fleeting images, might-have-beens. But his son didn't care. Jeff didn't have a gun and had come only to walk with Sam as his father hunted. They stood looking down into the valley where the foothills folded into each other.

"These people saw the murder?" Sam asked, his lip quivering.

"It's possible but not likely."

Sam studied the workers in the distance and took a deep breath. "Why's that?"

"These are migrant workers, hired to harvest the crop." Haddon pointed to a series of lean-tos at the far end "That's where they're staying. The rice crop matures at different times in different parts of the country. These people work wherever the harvest is happening. It's not very likely this group was involved in the transplanting. More likely the farmers themselves or other migrant workers."

"So it might have been local people who actually saw it happen?" Sam asked, feeling more in control.

"Yes, but don't expect much cooperation. After all, by the time the neighbours came to take him to the hospital, he'd been stripped of his watch, ring, wallet, shoes, and who knows what else."

Sam gritted his teeth but said nothing.

"So if you do manage to talk to them, you'd better forget that ever happened."

"Why did they do that?"

Haddon smiled grimly. "You've worked with disadvantaged people. Sometimes when opportunities present themselves..."

Sam nodded. He looked away from the fields and began studying the ground around them, not sure what he expected to find. Then he looked at the stone with the garlands. "Is that for Jeff?"

"In a manner of speaking. It's for his spirit, so he won't come back and haunt the place."

The two men went back to watching the workers in

silence.

"You know that discussion we had earlier about changing the system instead of the hearts?" Haddon asked.

"Yes?"

"Your son's position on that one was closer to yours than mine."

CHAPTER TWELVE

The air conditioning at the airport catered to foreigners. The Thais were all wearing sweaters or coats. She had been in hotels and department stores in downtown Bangkok where the temperature had been set this low. She had even willed herself to spend time in such places, thinking it would give her the experience of what it was like to live in Sweden or America or Germany. When she got too cold, she left. Now there was no place to go, not for a few more hours, anyway.

She studied the computer screen above the baggage check-in and found what she wanted. If anyone asked, she would say that she had just come in from Chiang Mai and was waiting for the eleven a.m. flight from Berlin. Her husband was German and she would be meeting the plane.

Chiang had no experience with German men, but she imagined them to be tall, strong, blond with deep blue eyes, and hopelessly devoted to their wives. She allowed herself to play with that fantasy for a while but the cold kept intruding. Then she went out the front door to where the taxis parked and stood warming herself for a short while amid the lingering exhaust fumes and other smells of the city. The drivers watched her from a distance, their cigarettes making little red traces in the night air and their muted discussions of her attributes occasionally audible. When it looked as though one of them was about to approach her, she turned and went back into the cold.

People were beginning to congregate near the doors for international arrivals. She looked at her watch. It was nearly three a.m., two and a half hours before the first buses would begin taking commuters into Bangkok. She was tired. There were nearly five hundred American dollars in her handbag, so she could afford a cab, providing they would take American money. She wasn't sure about that. Then she remembered the way the drivers had looked at her and talked about her. They were contemptible. She turned her attention back to those waiting and to the doors beyond them. Perhaps he would come through those doors, her foreign savior. Perhaps she would not have to find him in the bars downtown.

* * *

Haddon brought the pickup to a stop in front of a building that reminded Sam of one of those cheap motels found in small prairie towns in the early sixties. It was long rectangle with many doors and large windows, all with the curtains drawn.

"This is the guesthouse," Haddon explained. I hope you don't mind. I booked us a room together. Had to. The place was pretty full. Haddon opened a door near the end of the building. Inside were two single beds, a desk, a wardrobe, and a large ceiling fan. No air conditioning. Except for the fan, it reminded Sam of a college dorm.

"I'm going to lie down for a couple of hours before lunch. After lunch, I'll be in a meeting for a while. Gladys Petrie is the matron here. I'm sure she'd be glad to show you around while we're in our meeting."

"So until then I'm on my own?"

"I suggest you rest as well, but if you want to explore, that's fine, too. I don't think you can get into too much trouble here." Haddon stepped back out into the sun and pointed. "See that shelter over there?"

Sam looked in the direction Haddon was pointing. He could see a roof over an otherwise open-air platform about one hundred meters away. A few people were sitting at tables in the shade. In the foreground, someone in a wheelchair was being pushed away from the shelter by a relative or friend.

"There's a really good view of the river from there. You might enjoy that."

"Thanks," Sam said. "I'll probably just go for a walk in the Thai sun. Any place around here where a person might get a cold drink?"

Haddon pointed. "Over by the hospital proper. There's a little open-air restaurant just to the left of the main doors."

With that, Haddon retired into the room and left Sam standing, hands in pockets, on the verandah of the guesthouse. From there he had a good view of most of the hospital complex. It had been built in increments over the past forty-five years, beginning with the donation of a rice field in the early fifties. Now its nearly three hundred beds occupied a zigzag of plain box concrete rectangles all about three stories in height. Support buildings, whose purposes ranged from power generation to occupational therapy, filled the niches between the main buildings. Further out were staff residences. Some were single-family houses for the medical missionaries and senior Thai staff, but most were dormitories for the nurses and other staff who wished to live on the hospital grounds. The grounds themselves were well kept, with large leafy hardwoods and flower gardens.

It was the largest private hospital in the country outside of Bangkok and the largest hospital of any kind in the Central region. Its existence, however, was in jeopardy due to a shortage of senior medical personal. The Thai government was no longer giving visas to foreign medical professionals, and while the country's university system was now generating enough doctors and nurses to fill the needs, few of these were Christians. The SOS had a policy of having only committed Christians in senior staff positions at the hospital and felt that to compromise this would seriously undermine the Christian character of the institution.

Sam shook his head. You don't abandon something like this because you can't get the people you want. What, after all, is Christian character? A set of values? Why not make those values the charter by which the institution operates and hire only people who agree with it? All you had to do was drop this absurd business of committing one's life to Christ.

He stepped off the verandah, squinted and lit a cigarette. The sun was coming up from behind the hospital. He could see people seated beneath a canopy to the left of the main entrance. All he wanted was a Coke. That should be simple enough.

Several people were sitting in the restaurant. They were either reading Thai newspapers or talking. No one was eating. Sam approached a young woman who seemed to be working there. "Coke," he said.

The woman looked at him blankly for a moment and then nodded. She walked toward a cooler at the far end of the restaurant. Another young woman was already there leaning against the machine. They both began to giggle and gesture in Sam's direction. At first Sam wondered if he had been misunderstood, but when the woman reached into the cooler and pulled out a bottle of Coke, he realized this wasn't the case. She walked back to him, found an opener, popped the top off the bottle, and then, to Sam's amazement, began pouring the contents into a small plastic bag. She inserted a straw into this and then tied the end with an elastic band. This done, she handed the bag to Sam.

"*Supe buri, tamai*?" she said.

Sam looked at her blankly, wondering how much he was being asked for.

"*Supe buri, tamai*?" she repeated gesturing to his cigarette.

Sam looked at his cigarette. She had probably never seen a Westerner smoke. The only Westerners at the hospital were missionaries. He smiled, gripped the cigarette with his mouth, and took his wallet out of his back pocket. "How much?" he asked.

"Fye *baht*," she said holding up the appropriate number of fingers.

Sam reached into his pocket, pulled out a five *baht* coin and handed it to the woman. She took it, gave him a smile that ended their interaction and walked back to her friend by the cooler. Both giggled.

Sam looked at the bag of Coke now suspended by an elastic band looped over two of the fingers on his left hand. "Two bits for a bottle of Coke," he said to himself. "Not bad, but you don't get the bottle." The elastic band appeared to be straining. He bounced the bag a couple of times tentatively. It held, but he decided to cup the bag with his right hand anyway. It was cold and already wet with condensation.

He began walking toward the shelter, holding the bag slightly away from his body, and allowing the half smoked cigarette to bounce lightly in his lips with each step. He thought of Buster Keaton. Did Keaton smoke on screen? He couldn't remember, but Keaton would have made a straight-faced sight gag out of this little walk.

The shelter was now empty. Whoever had been there was gone. Sam would not be on display. He sat down on a bench, took the cigarette out of his mouth, and put the straw in. He drank half of the bag without stopping. It was much sweeter than Coke in Canada. He took one last draw on the cigarette and then ground it out under the heel of his sandal. He watched it until the smoldering stopped and his eyes found the brown river below.

> Punctuality was not Jeff's forte but it was a near-obsession with Sam, even when he knew that the other half of the appointment was likely to be late. I'm setting a good example, he told himself, but his son never seemed to notice. Sam took a cigarette from his pack and lit it. I'm not setting a good example, he corrected himself, but Jeff had never picked up on his smoking, either. The woman at the next table gave him a disapproving look. His table was in the smoking section, but right on the border. Hers was on the other side of the line. She wore a dress of wrinkled unbleached cotton and pounds of jewelry that could have passed for armor. Sam decided to ignore her.

Simpatico Restaurant was not his favorite place. The food and the coffee were good, but the place was frequented by artists, hippies, and other such oddballs, about half of whom seemed to be hopped up on something. He was forever resisting the temptation to get up and bust someone. He was also sure that everyone knew he was a cop. I smoke like a cop, he told himself. He glanced again at the woman at the next table. She was now holding a handkerchief over her face. He put out the cigarette.

"You didn't have to put that out for me," Jeff said, taking the seat across from his father.

"I was not putting it out because of you. I was getting tired of smoking,"

"Good sign," Jeff said. "Sorry I'm late. Missed the bus."

"They run every ten minutes. You must have missed three buses."

"Yeah, I missed three." Jeff grinned at his father.

"So, how's it going?"

Jeff hesitated a moment before answering. "Great, Dad!" he said. The "great" was bigger than it should have been.

"Something the matter, Jeff?"

"No Dad. Everything's great, just like I said."

Sam took another cigarette out of the package and started to light it. “So, tell me about it,” he said.

Jeff hesitated again for a moment. “Let's order first. I'm famished.”

They both ordered steak sandwiches. He likes to conform to my eating habits, Sam thought. It's his way of cementing the relationship. But Jeff's conformity to his father had gone beyond that. He was at the police academy studying to be a cop.

“So what's great in your life?” Sam asked.

“Well,” Jeff hesitated, “do you know a guy named Tony Cecconi? He's one of the instructors at the school.”

“I know him. We were in vice together a few years back.”

“Well, he's involved in this organization called Canadian Fellowship of Peace Officers. Have you heard of it?”

“Yeah, at least I think so...It's a club for religious cops or something. I didn't know he was involved in that.”

Jeff played with his napkin and then took a drink of water. “He invited me over to his place a couple of Wednesdays back. There were half a dozen cops there and their wives.” He shrugged. “One of the guys got up and basically told the story of his life, including how he became a Christian. I mean, it was okay. I usually feel manipulated when somebody does that kind of thing to me. But it was a nice story, you know. I liked the guy. I liked what he had to say. So later on, when Tony asked me if I wanted to go to church with him and his wife, I said sure." Jeff stopped and looked at his father.

"Go on," Sam said after a silence.

"The church was right down on Nelson by your place. First Baptist. Do you know it?"

Sam nodded. "Fine old building. I've walked past it many times."

"Ever been inside it?"

Sam shook his head. "Not my scene, Jeff. You know that."

"Well, anyway, I went with them. To an evening service, an evangelistic service." Jeff paused and licked his lips. "I liked what I heard, Dad, I believed it."

Sam studied his son for a moment. "So what are you trying to say, Jeff?"

"That I believe, Dad. That I've become a Christian."

Sam raised his eyebrows. "You had plenty of opportunities to do that as a kid. Why now?"

"Well Mom was always kind of pushy about it. Know what I mean? But this was different, more relaxed. I had time to think about it."

Sam nodded. "Good, a little religion never hurt anybody."

"It's not that simple, Dad. It's not like just changing your mind about something. This is a complete life-changing thing. I mean, accepting Jesus as your personal Savior is not like changing your suit, you know."

Sam shook his head. "Jeff, just give it some time, Okay? Just give it some time. What seems tremendously important right now tends to get a bit more balance after a while. You'll see."

Balance! That kid never knew the meaning of the word!

Sam finished the last of his Coke and looked for a garbage can. There was none available. Instead the area was strewn with plastic bags, paper, and other bits of junk. These clung to the plants and bushes that rushed down the steep slope to the river. *Why did Jeff think this place was so beautiful? How could he have not noticed the garbage?* Sam shuddered. His son had only seen the river. Jeff had only seen the river.

* * *

Lup Law studied the face of his lieutenant. Kwanchai had been spending too much time in the sun since buying a mango orchard earlier in the year. His skin was now dark, but it suited him. He was a farmer at heart and he loved his trees, but he was not a good cop. He didn't like being in the thick of things and was non-confrontational to the extreme. He couldn't shoot worth a damn and he was a poor leader of men. These traits didn't sit well with his subordinates, all of whom wanted Kwanchai's promotion. He had three qualities, however, that made him indispensable to Lup Law.

The first was Kwanchai's intense loyalty. He was on Lup Law's side and wasn't on anyone else's. His second indispensable quality was his lack of ambition. His trees were more important to him than his position. His third and most important quality was his ability always to know what was going on. He was a friendly, easy-going man in whom people liked to confide, and he always seemed to have information an hour or two before anyone else.

"Well, what have you got for me?"

Kwanchai gave his superior a weak smile. "Well, we know she didn't get off at the main terminal because we had a half-dozen people watching the train. And she didn't get off at Samsen and transfer to a southbound train, because that station was watched, too."

Lup Law fingered the amulet around his neck. A thin smile grew on his lips. "She bought a ticket to the main terminal knowing that I would find out about that. Funny, I never gave her that much credit but, after all, she is my daughter, isn't she?" He pulled the amulet from around his neck and looked at it. "Get someone out to the airport."

"The airport?"

"Yes, it's the last place I would look for her and she knows that." Lup Law looked at his watch. "And you'd better hurry. The buses will be going from there into Bangkok in less than an hour."

"Yes, Sir," Kwanchai said, but he didn't move.

"Well?"

"I just thought you'd like to know that Jep's father is here."

"His father?"

"From Canada. He's a Canadian police officer. Apparently he's here to find his son's killer."

Lup Law looked at Kwanchai blankly. "How did you find that out?"

"I have a friend who meets with the Christians in Khoksamrong. They had a meeting last night and..."

Lup Law waved his hand. "Never mind, just go and see about the airport."

Kwanchai bowed and left his superior again fingering his amulet. Lup Law looked out of his window to the water reservoir across the street from the police station. It was a large open cement pool where children played and sometimes drowned, two in the last year. Still, there was no fence and no plans to put one up. Bad karma. That was the problem. The children had bad karma. Nothing you could do about that.

Lup Law began to wonder about his own karma. In the past eight hours his daughter had run off, his only son had told him that he had no intention of ever leaving the Buddhist monkhood, and now Jep's police officer father was here to investigate his son's murder.

* * *

During the course of the night, Chiang watched people arrive at the airport from eleven different flights. There were two each from England, Hong Kong, and America; and flights from Saudi Arabia, Australia, Germany, Holland and India. Except for the flight from Saudi Arabia, there were attractive Western men on every flight. She did nothing but watch them walk through the terminal. How does one approach a man in a place like this? When it got close to dawn she picked up her bag and began walking to the bus stop.

The airport was far enough out so, when the buses began to run, it was still possible to get a seat. Chiang passed the air conditioned bus that showed up first. She'd had enough of air conditioning during the night. The second bus that came was nearly empty but it was going to Thonburi, not the part of the city she had in mind. Still, empty seats on city buses were rare and would make it easier to protect her bag. A certain randomness was desirable when it came to eluding her father and finding a place in Thonburi shouldn't be too difficult.

She took a seat by the window and toward the front of the bus. She had barely seated herself when a wave of weariness nearly overcame her. To be on the safe side she wrapped the strap of her bag around her ankle several times. That way, if she fell asleep, no one could take the bag without waking her. Then she allowed her head to lean against the side of the open window.

* * *

"This," said Gladys Petrie, with a gesture intended to take in all of the sixteen-bed hospital room, "is where it all started for us here. Not just the room itself but also the people in it."

The room in front of Sam was basic in the extreme. The walls were painted light green and there were two rows of eight beds on either side of the room. There were windows and storage cabinets but little else, certainly nothing that one would normally associate with a hospital room. There were no electric devices of any kind, save for a single radio on one of the cabinets. The room was devoid even of those little button devices used to call the nurse. But Gladys Petrie was right. It was the people who made the room unique.

Only two of them were in beds, their plastered appendages resting on pillows. The rest sat on a collection of straw mats in the large open centre of the room. These folks, too, were plastered to varying degrees but looked healthy otherwise, once you got beyond the obvious damage left by their disease. Most gave Sam a cheery smile. Several had open Bibles in front of them.

"Most of these folks are on the margins of Thai society. Before we came into their lives they were shunned by everyone, including the medical community. If you're a leper in this society, you must have terrible karma. You must have done something truly awful in a past life to reap such a reward. So, no one would help them. The conventional wisdom was that they should be left to work through their karma. Then we came along and took care of them. We treated them as we believed Christ would have. That's why so many of them are Christians."

Gladys Petrie gestured to the people in the room. "These folks are recovering from reconstructive surgery. We do what we can to make their limbs function a little better. A lot of the damage is irreversible, but sometimes only a small improvement will give them a lot more mobility. If we can give them back some use of a hand, then it may be possible for them to begin earning a living again."

"Doing what?" Sam asked.

"Well, that's the big question, of course." Gladys Petrie paused to consider her answer. She reminded Sam of his mother as she was in her the early fifties. Same graying backcombed hairstyle and loose midi dress. Same varicose veins. He could imagine Gladys puttering around in his mother's kitchen back in Saskatoon and he bringing Alice home to meet her. The trouble was this was the 1980s. The 1950s was about the time Gladys would have arrived out here, if Sam was any judge of age. Had she lost touch with everything that had happened since then?

"We teach print-making, shoe repair, and weaving in the occupational therapy unit out back," Gladys finally said. "There are some government programs that they can get into. Mostly those are just traditional Thai crafts, business courses, and academic upgrading—a surprising number of them just go back into farming. It's the only thing they know."

"I'll bet most of them don't do much of anything."

"Well, I admit there's some truth in that. Nearly all of these people have spent most of their lives seeing themselves as thoroughly beaten and defeated. It's a hard self-image to overcome." She looked glum and then brightened. "But, as you can see, they have a future in Heaven to look forward to. I guess that makes it all worthwhile."

"I guess." Sam studied the cheery faces of the people again. Life had dealt them a truly bad hand but you'd never know it. Perhaps Jeff had been doing some good out here.

CHAPTER THIRTEEN

"Blind?" Sam's look was incredulous. "Are you telling me that the man you found to translate for me is blind?"

Haddon pursed his lips, looked down and then returned to meet Sam's gaze. "Since birth. He's never experienced sight."

Sam's mouth opened, tried the beginnings of several words and then closed. He took a deep breath. "Look Haddon, I'm here to investigate my son's murder, an investigation your mission has made it very clear it wants no part of—"

"He's the best English speaker of any Thai I know."

"I'm sure he is, but that's hardly the point, and you know it! He won't be able to read the road signs. How will we get anywhere?"

"There are road signs in English for any place you'll need to go. Besides, he can ask directions if need be. He also knows many of the people that Jeff knew because he spent some time working as an interpreter at the hospital. Not while Jeff was in Banmi, but a few years back. That should be useful, because he knows his way around the area. I should also point out that we've used a lot of interpreters over the years in this mission and all the others were sighted. There's no question in my mind that Larry was the best of the lot despite his limitations."

Sam shook his head. "Get serious, Haddon. I need someone who can take me around. Not someone I have to lead around. And there are going to be a lot of things I'll want read. How am I going to get that done?"

Haddon took a sheaf of papers out of his brief case and set it on the table before Sam. "I've translated all the relevant newspaper articles for you. There haven't been any now for over two months—things have kind of died down—and I don't think you'll find them very useful, but here they are."

"When did you do this?"

"I started working on it a couple of weeks ago when we heard you were coming. They're pretty rough, I'm afraid, but the gist of everything is there."

"Why didn't you give them to me when I first arrived?"

"I was hoping it wouldn't be necessary."

"You actually expected me to leave here without doing anything?"

"Stranger things have happened, especially out here."

Sam picked up the papers and looked at them. "What about police reports?"

Haddon sighed. "This isn't Canada, Mr. Watson. What gets into the police reports is what they want in there, not what actually happened. I'm sure you can get access to them if you push the right buttons, maybe even in English. They'll want it to look like they're cooperating. I'm equally sure they'll be virtually useless to you. Anyway, Larry can get someone to read them to him and he can translate."

There was a long pause during which Sam studied Haddon's resolute face. "You're not going to find me another translator, are you?"

"Mr. Watson I have a lot of responsibilities in this organization, a lot of things I have to get done. I've been at your disposal for nearly a week now and rightfully so because I was your son's supervisor and I cared about him very much, but that has put me way behind in my work. I chose Larry because he's good, he's available, he knows something of the context in which you'll be working, and he's cheap. He's also mature in terms of how he handles responsibility and that may well be his biggest asset in this country. I think you should at least meet him."

Sam looked long and hard at Haddon. "When?"

"I can get him here this afternoon."

Sam stood up. "Fine. Let's get it over with."

* * *

Mekong whiskey was harsh and crude. This was new knowledge for Nak, gained after two months of indulging in Jack Daniels. When the money from the killing of the *farang* was gone, he was forced to return to his old standby. It soured and burned in a mouth reoriented to a finer taste, but it did the trick.

All this was beyond the experience of his companion, Bua Tong, a brown and chipped-toothed pedicab driver whose skin wore an ever-expanding collection of tattoos for the warding-off of demons. Like his whiskey, Nak's companions were now of lesser quality.

Bua Tong waited, grinning, for the next fill from Nak's bottle. He waited because Nak drank slowly, preferring to taste what was in his mouth before swallowing. Bua Tong poured the stuff directly down his throat. Nak wanted to experience the journey, however rough. Bua Tong only wanted to be there. Nak poured his friend another drink and watched as it immediately disappeared. If this was Jack Daniels, Bua Tong would never know it.

Nak became dimly aware of two light-brown uniforms standing beside his table. He looked up.

"Lup Law wants to see you," the officer said without introduction.

"The police captain?"

"That's the one."

"Have I done something? Am I under arrest?"

"We were told to find you and tell you that he wanted to see you. No one said anything about arresting you."

"Oh, well then it can't be too important," Nak said and poured himself another drink.

The two police officers didn't move.

"Well?" said Nak after a moment of unpleasant silence.

"He wants to see you now."

* * *

There were several missionaries in the parking lot, all of whom seemed to know the small blind man Haddon was leading from the pickup. Sam watched an enthusiastic exchange of greetings from the other side of the blinds in the guesthouse. The man wore sunglasses, moved his hands awkwardly, and took small steps not unlike those of a stroke victim learning to walk again. There was no white cane.

After a moment, Sam realized that the man would not be aware of his presence even if he were in full view. He stepped out the door on to the verandah. Haddon noticed him at once.

"Come on, Larry. The man I want you to meet is on the verandah. You can catch up with the others later. They'll be back for supper."

“Where are you going?” Larry called out as five missionaries began cramming themselves into a Toyota taxi.

“To a meeting at the pubs,” one of them answered.

Sam raised an eyebrow in Haddon's direction.

“The publishers,” Haddon said. “We publish Christian books in Thai on a small scale. These folks are part of a council that decides what should be published. When we translate English books, Larry's usually part of the process.”

Sam took a long hard look at Larry. He was dressed in cotton pants and a yellowish paisley shirt, the left front tail of which was untucked. His shoes were the usual plastic sandals, he had a slight stoop, and his hands made small involuntary movements that pleaded for a piano.

“Don't get lost,” Larry shouted, but the taxi was already moving down the driveway.

“Larry, I want you to meet Sam Watson,” Haddon said.

Larry extended his hand cautiously and Sam grasped it. He felt it go limp.

“Pleased to meet you, Mr. Watson,” Larry said, his voice sounding froggy, almost adolescent.

“Pleased to meet you, Larry,” Sam said as firm-voiced as he could manage.

There was an awkward pause during which Sam released Larry's hand. The hand resumed its keyboard playing movements. Sam looked at Haddon who said “It’s involuntary I think.”

“Am I doing the hand thing again?” Larry said.

“Yes, you are,” said Haddon.

“Sorry.” Larry dropped his hands to his sides.

"Well, let's go inside then, shall we?" Haddon said. "I'll see if I can find us something cold to drink."

Haddon led the shuffling Larry into the large open living room of the guesthouse and deposited him in a corner of the sofa. Sam chose a chair opposite as Haddon went for the drinks.

"I didn't hear about Jeff's death until it was too late to go to the funeral," Larry said. "That's one of the disadvantages of listening to the BBC all the time. I miss the local news."

Larry's English was nothing like the English Sam had heard spoken by other Thais. "You sound pretty American for someone who listens to the BBC," Sam said.

Larry laughed. "Well, I listen to the Voice of America quite a bit, too. And most of the taped books I have were read by people with American accents." He switched to a BBC English accent. "I can do most English accents if I've been exposed to them often enough. I don't get much exposure to Canadian speakers. I taught Thai to Jeff when he first came out here. But the time was too short for me to learn to speak with a Canadian accent. There's supposed to be a Canadian short-wave service broadcasting out here now, but I haven't been able to find it on the dial." He switched accents again. "I thought you might be more comfortable with an American accent since it's closer to home, but I'll do BBC if you like."

Sam looked at the funny little man sitting across from him and judged him to be in his late twenties, perhaps early thirties. "One or the other but not both," he said.

Haddon entered the room with a tray of iced Cokes and cookies, distributed them, and then sat down on the opposite end of the sofa.

"What kind of interpreting work have you done in the past, Larry?" Sam asked.

"Well, most of it's been with missionaries or mission organizations. SOS is the main one, I suppose. But I also worked for a while with a travel agency."

"What did you do there?"

"At first I was a general interpreter, helping with English-speaking tourists, but after awhile I was just assigned to answer the phone." Larry abruptly sat on his hands. "I have some mannerisms that others find distracting. It's hard to know how people are reacting to you if you can't see."

"Do you play the piano?"

"I wish, but I could never afford one. Probably just as well, because in this climate you need an air conditioner and a humidifier to keep them in tune. I don't have that, either. Maybe someday I'll get an electronic keyboard."

Sam looked at Haddon, who said nothing. "Do you get enough work to earn a living, Larry?" Sam asked .

"Not lately. Most of my clients are mission agencies and they haven't needed my services in the last while. So I've just been staying at home with my parents. I get a little money from the government if I sell lottery tickets, which I don't do often." He paused and then brightened. "I understand SOS may have a new doctor coming in from the States, so I may be able to help there."

"What am I going to have to do for you, Larry?"

"Do?"

"I haven't got much experience working with the blind."

"Oh," Larry considered the question. "You have to be my eyes when I need eyes. You have to lead me when we go places."

Sam looked at Haddon and their eyes met. "Do you know why I'm here? What the work involves?" he asked Larry, his eyes still on Haddon.

Larry responded slowly. "I had a talk with Stuart."

"Well?"

"He said you wanted to find the person who killed your son." Larry looked uncomfortable.

"How do you feel about that?"

"Of course one likes to see justice done. I just don't see how you will succeed where the Thai police have failed."

Sam looked at Haddon again. "I don't have an answer for that, but I do know this. The SOS has decided they don't want to be involved in the investigation. They feel it will threaten their position here. I don't know enough about the way things work out here to know whether or not that's true. But I'm willing to give them the benefit of the doubt and assume that it is. And if it is, then maybe they have a good reason to stay out of it. It means weighing justice off against self-preservation. That's a hard decision, but I guess if you think your organization is doing worthwhile work out here, you're going to opt for self-preservation. But for me, seeking justice wins out. I'm a cop, so that stands to reason, I guess. And the victim was my son. So I want to cooperate where the SOS felt it couldn't. Maybe that additional cooperation will make a difference. I don't know. But at least this way it doesn't involve the SOS, not directly, anyway. And I have a very good reason for being here on my own."

"And do you know that the police here are not the same as the police back in Canada?"

"The corruption, you mean?"
"Yes."
"Yeah, I've heard about that."
"And do you understand that there may be corruption involved in this case? That the police may actually have been involved in Jeff's killing?"
"You mean the police may have had him killed?"
"It's possible. Or, it's possible that they know who did it and have been paid off not to arrest him. In this country all that a criminal needs to do is make it profitable for the police not to arrest him."
"Are all the cops dishonest here?"
"No, but those who aren't usually fear those who are."
"Are you saying I'm beaten before I get started?"
"No. But I think you need to be aware of the obstacles."
Sam sighed. "I'm becoming more aware all the time."
"There is one thing in your favour," Larry said.
"What's that?"
"Somebody is trying to save face."
"Save face?"
Larry's hands began their piano-playing movements again. "They are trying to find someone. When Jeff was first killed, they said they knew who had done it, and they were looking for him. If the police had killed him or if they had been paid off, they would not look very hard. They would just say that they didn't know who had done it and had no leads. Nothing much would happen. But they said it was the police captain's son-in-law. They said he killed Jeff because Jeff was sleeping with his wife. Obviously the police captain doesn't like his son-in-law or else everything would have been buried soon after the investigation started. They thought they could find him

easily, but the son-in-law has disappeared. They are still actively searching for him. I know this because I have friends in the church at Khoksamrong and they have been watching things. All of this means that the police captain is losing face. He must find his son-in-law or be embarrassed in public."

"Do you think my son slept with the son-in-law's wife?"

Larry sat on his hands. "It isn't the kind of thing a good Christian man would do, and only a fool would sleep with the daughter of a police captain. Jeff was a good Christian and he was no fool."

"And do you think the son-in-law did it?"

"He picked an odd time to disappear."

Haddon shifted his position on the sofa.

Sam looked at Haddon. "You don't think he did it?"

Haddon shook his head. "The stories the neighbours told about Jeff's meetings with the daughter were a bit too contrived. I was personally with Jeff on one occasion when they were supposed to have been involved in this passion. The stories sound very much like inventions after the fact."

"The question is whether the son-in-law thought something was going on," Sam said. He turned to Larry. "How much is this going to cost me?"

Larry grinned. "A Casio," he said.

"A Casio? What's a Casio?" Sam said.

Haddon looked at Larry in amazement. "He wants a keyboard, an electronic keyboard. They're about six thousand *baht*, about three hundred dollars. He's being a bit cheeky, I'm afraid."

Sam looked at Larry and smiled. "So what was that song you were playing?" he asked.

"Do you know Chick Corea?"
"Can't say I do."
"Then you wouldn't know the song."

* * *

Nak sat stiffly on the chair across from Lup Law's desk in the captain's office. He watched through a Mekong whiskey haze as the police captain fingered the amulet around his neck. It was a powerful charm. Nak knew the maker, a spirit doctor from Saraburi province who lived near the temple where there was a footprint of the Lord Buddha. The maker was known all over Thailand as a man of great power. His amulets were expensive.

The captain was also talking about the job Nak had done and his own frustration at not being able to find his son-in-law. The talk had a rhythm and an eloquence that Nak admired. The captain was a good talker, a good talker with a powerful amulet. That's why he was captain. That's why everyone was afraid of him. He was a good talker with a great amulet and he was talking to Nak. Nak smiled.

"I came to an agreement with your employer, as you know. But a few problems have come up. The first is that I have not found my son-in-law, and the second is that you drink too much and when you do that you are not careful in what you say. Several people in town now believe that it was you who killed the missionary."

"Who cares what they believe?" Nak shrugged.

"You should understand that there's nothing I can do if you insist on pointing the finger at yourself. And there is another thing that you should know. The father of the missionary is now in Thailand. He is a police officer from Canada and he has come to find his son's killer. He will make no agreements. But more importantly, I will not have him succeed where I have failed."

"He is a foreigner. He doesn't speak Thai. How can he do what you have not been able to do?"

Lup Law fingered his amulet and smiled. "You forget, Mr. Hired Killer, that I know who the murderer is. So, apparently, do a number of other people. All he has to do is ask the right person and..." Lup Law made an expansive gesture. "But don't worry. I won't allow that to happen. I'll have you in custody long before he gets near you. Unless of course you're able to find my son-in-law."

"Me? You want me to find... But if the entire police department can't find him, how am I supposed to?"

"Sometimes a small machine can do a job that a large machine cannot."

Nak felt the color drain from his face. Lup Law fastened the amulet back around his neck and dismissed Nak with a wave of his hand. Nak walked slowly down to ground level and out into the parking lot.

CHAPTER FOURTEEN

A trail of ants led down the side of the rail car's window and disappeared into an ashtray that was mounted just below it. The bone end of a mostly eaten chicken leg protruded from this, a feast for the insects that seemed undeterred by the ash that Sam dropped on them every few moments.

Across from him, stretched out as fully as the seat would allow, Larry slept. He had never ridden second-class on the train before and was determined to enjoy it to the fullest. He'd strapped a set of headphones over his ears and listened in a state of comfort and bliss until, with a few barely perceptible nods, the midday heat caught up with him. Now, for the first time since their initial meeting several days earlier, Larry looked normal.

Apart from Larry there were only four other passengers in the car, a middle-aged man dressed in a Western-style suit and three sleeping police officers. In the distance Sam saw the same *Khmer* ruins he'd seen earlier with Haddon as the train pulled into Lopburi station. He nudged Larry.

"*Bye looy!*" Larry said trying to ignore him.

"Larry, we're pulling into Lopburi. It's time to get off."

"*Arai*? Oh, yes, of course." Larry's hands fumbled in his lap until he found his tape machine, which he turned off, and his sunglasses, which he put on. He stood up, feeding the tape machine and the headphones into the soft bag that hung from his shoulder. "You get your suitcase and then give me the strap from it. You can pull me along with that just like we did in the terminal in Bangkok."

Sam picked up the suitcase and fed the strap into Larry's hand. The train slowed to a stop and he led Larry down the steps and helped him onto the platform. The two of them stood there silently while the boarding passengers pushed by them. In less than two minutes, the train was on its way again.

"Now what?" Sam asked.

"We find the hotel." Larry said, still holding the strap to the suitcase. "Stuart said it was in the north part of town near the government buildings. He didn't know the name of it, though, just that it was new and built for Westerners, for tourists."

"So how do we do that?"

"We wait. Someone will come."

Even as Larry spoke Sam noticed a man walking with determination toward them. He wore green shorts, a torn red and blue Pepsi T-shirt, blue rubber sandals, and a yellow Mack truck baseball cap. He was thin, wiry, and bow-legged.

"*Pai nai khrap*?" the man said.

"*Pai rong rem mi nak tong teo*," Larry replied. "*Mi rote arai?*"

"*Ooy, my mi rote. Mi samlaw,*" the man said, shaking his head.

They continued to talk for a minute or so. Then the man bowed to Sam and left them.

"It's always the pedicab drivers who get to you first," Larry said. "He says the hotel is too far for him to take us so he's gone to get a friend who has a taxi. It'll cost about twenty *baht* to get there."

"Sounds good," Sam said.

After a few moments, the thin man reappeared with a taller, stockier man who wore long navy-blue pants and a floral print shirt. His hair was greased back and he was smoking a cigarette. The man and Larry talked.

"He wants thirty-five *baht* to take you," Larry said.

"I thought you said twenty *baht*?"

"It's because you're a foreigner. He says he always charges the tourists fifty *baht*. He says he's giving you a deal."

"But that's..."

"Unfair? Racist, maybe? It just the way things work. He's only charging what he thinks you will pay. Tourists have more money than the local people so he charges them more. To him, it's just good business."

"Tell him I'm not a tourist. Tell him I'm a police officer."

"You are a Westerner. All Westerners are rich."

Sam looked at the two Thai men in front of them. It was hard to argue with the logic and the sandals on his feet were bothering him. "And what if I refuse to pay?"

"It's a long walk."

"All right," Sam said nodding at the driver.

The man picked up Sam's suitcase and staggered along with it through the station and into the small parking lot out back. He threw the bag into the back of a small Isuzu vehicle that looked like a miniature flatbed trunk. This had a canopy over the back and two benches no more than six inches off the floor. The man gestured to them that this was where they should sit.

"You're kidding?" Sam said.

"What?" said Larry.

"He wants us to sit in the back of some kind of pickup. Almost on the floor!"

"Help me up," Larry said. "Taxis up country are not the same as they are in Bangkok. Out here anyone who makes his living with a vehicle must own one that can do many things."

Sam shook his head and helped Larry on to the truck. Larry sat down on the bench and folded his legs beneath him as if he was sitting flat on the floor. Then Sam got in, lowered himself onto a bench, and stretched his legs out. The driver closed the gate behind them.

* * *

It took Nak about half an hour before he realized, in his alcohol haze, that he was being followed. It was even fairly obvious, now that he was aware of it. The two officers kept to within twenty-five meters of him and made no attempt to hide their presence. What had they seen so far? They had watched him buy a pack of cigarettes from a vendor near the police station and then, a little further down the street, buy a bag of fried bananas from another cart. He then wandered around downtown Banmi, smoking, munching, and trying to think through his options.

One of those options was now gone, or at least would be considerably more difficult, that of disappearing. Ute had done it. But Ute was not being followed. Or, perhaps he was. Maybe that was what tipped him off to disappear in the first place. So if one is being followed, how does one disappear? Go to a busy place, a place with lots of people milling about and give them the slip. That should be easy. But there was no such busy place in Banmi, not at this time of the day, anyway. The morning market was an option, but that was twelve hours from now. Nak shook his head. Even if he did give them the slip at the market they'd have all the ways out of town covered within minutes.

Nak found himself walking toward the village on the outskirts of town where Ute and Chiang had their house. He wasn't sure which house it was, but the neighbours would know. Nak looked behind him. The two officers were still there, but now one of them had a motorcycle. Where did that come from? he wondered. The other officer walked along with his hand resting awkwardly on his gun holster.

Nak thought of his own gun, carefully hidden beneath the floorboards of a friend's house. It was in the opposite direction from where he was going. He could beat the officers behind him. He was fairly certain of that, but it would make him the enemy of every cop in the country and they would get him eventually.

A man passed them herding a half-dozen scrawny white cows. He looked at Nak curiously. I must be a sight, thought Nak, walking through this village with a police escort.

"Could you tell me where the house that belongs to the police captain's daughter is?" he asked the man.

"Why not ask your friends?" the man said with a grin. "They know."

Nak looked back at his escort. Both men were grinning at him.

"Well?" he said.

"Just around the bend and down the lane to the right," said the officer on the motorcycle. "The lane comes to an end right in front of the house."

Lup Law had done nothing to protect his daughter's and

her husband's possessions. Anything of value that had once been in the house was gone, and part of the wood that made up the back of the house had also been salvaged.

Nak walked up the steps that led to the front of the house and pushed the door open. Inside, a thin layer of dust had settled on everything, disturbed only by *cheechak* tracks. A couple of old mats were still stacked in the corner and a few yellowing magazines lay scattered on the floor. Nothing else remained save for a few family pictures and a postcard, all of which were tacked to one of the support beams. Nak studied these carefully, not sure of what he expected to find.

The family pictures were just that, color and black-and-white photographs of family members from both sides. A touched-up color photograph of Lup Law from before he became a captain was among them. Another was of Ute's father, a minor official in the land titles office in Lopburi before his death. None of the photographs, as far as Nak could tell, would be of any use in determining Ute's whereabouts.

The postcard had a picture of a sandy beach and some writing in English that Nak couldn't read. He reached out, removed the tack and turned the card over. "Hello from Hua Hin. Making lots of money. Come visit," it said in Thai. The card was signed by someone called Bom. Nak studied the stamp. It had been canceled, but the job had been done quickly and the ink was smeared. It was impossible to tell when the card had been mailed. Still, it was a lead and one that Lup Law had apparently missed.

"You guys fancy a trip to the beach?" he said to the two uniformed observers.

* * *

The hotel was new unadorned white cement, air-conditioned but otherwise basic in what it offered. It had opened only a few weeks earlier and many of the rooms still had not been used. They put Sam and Larry into one of these at a cost of 250 *baht*.

A thin layer of white dust lay on the desk and chair, and also on the backboards of the two single beds. Sam suspected that this was from drywall, since the hallway was still unfinished. Sam looked at the bellboy and then spoke to Larry. "Tell him the room needs to be dusted and vacuumed if we're going to stay in here."

Larry relayed the information to the bellboy who nodded and then disappeared down the hallway. Sam put the suitcase in the corner and then led Larry to the room's only available chair. He looked around. There was no television, radio, or phone. The bathroom had a sink, mirror, a Western-style toilet, and a shower head that came out of a wall tiled to a height of about six feet. The tiles extended the entire circumference of the room and water exited by means of a drain in the middle of the floor. There was no tub or water reservoir.

"It's basic but it will do. Are you sure they don't have anything like this in Banmi?" Sam asked.

Larry shook his head. "There might be a hotel of sorts but it would be for Thais and would not have the things you'd expect. No private washrooms or Western style beds and toilets. And they wouldn't know what to do with you. Your needs would be very different from their normal clients."

"This will be our base of operations, then. At least for

the time being." Sam looked at his watch. It was nearly one in the afternoon. "How long did you say it would take to get to Banmi from here?"

"It's about half an hour by bus or twenty minutes by train. The bus might be easier from here and it's certainly more frequent. I'll have to ask where to get on, though. The train's more comfortable, but then you have to get to and from the station."

"The bus, then. Let's stow the luggage and find somewhere to eat. Then we'll find out where to catch the bus."

The bus stop turned out to be right across the street from the hotel. There was no shade though, and after about ten minutes of waiting, Sam was covered in sweat. It didn't help that his stomach was also a mess. At the hotel's restaurant, he had forced himself to eat a disgusting concoction that the menu called "American Fried Rice." This turned out to be regular fried rice soaked in ketchup.

The bus that finally arrived was one of those Orange Crush specials that Sam had first seen ensnared in traffic outside the airport in Bangkok. There was no crush on this day. Sam took Larry by the hand and led him slowly to some empty seats near the back. Every eye followed them.

"You take the window seat," Sam said when they arrived at an empty bench.

"You forget that I can't see."

"My legs are much too long to fit comfortably in there. I'm going to need to extend into the aisle."

Larry laughed. "They don't build Thai buses for Caucasian legs."

"Caucasian legs? How do you know I'm Caucasian?"

A look of horror spread over Larry's face. "You mean you're not? I thought Canada..."

"Was a white nation? The part of Canada where I live is almost twenty percent Asian."

"And you're..."

"The name Watson isn't very common among the Chinese," Sam said, now feeling cheap.

Larry pulled his bag into his lap and said nothing. Sam sat down beside him and allowed his legs to extend into the aisle.

An old woman in the seat in front of them turned and smiled. Sam gave a little gasp. Her gums were almost black and her teeth were bright red.

"What's wrong?" Larry asked.

"Oh, it's probably nothing," Sam said. "A woman just turned and smiled at me. She had black gums and red teeth."

"Probably chews *mak*."

"*Mak*?"

"I'm trying to remember the English word for it," Larry said. "Betel nut. That's it. She probably chews betel nut."

"Betel nut?"

"It's a mild narcotic. It's used mainly by older women in the villages. The young people don't use it much these days."

"I'm not surprised."

The woman was still smiling at Sam. He smiled back. She held up something that looked like a small ball of leaves. "*Ow mak mai kha*?" she said. A number of people on the bus laughed.

"What did she say?" Sam asked Larry.

"She was offering you some betel nut."

"Oh," Sam shook his head. There was more laughter.

"*Pai nai kha*?" the woman said.

"She wants to know where you're going," Larry said.

"Banmi," Sam said.

"*Tamai*?"

Sam looked at Larry, who said nothing.

"Well, what did she say?"

"She wants to know why."

"Tell her."

"Tell her what?"

"Tell her that I'm a Canadian police officer and that I'm going to Banmi to investigate the murder of my son."

"Tell her all that?"

"Yes."

"It would not be wise to do that."

"Just tell her. Maybe she knows something."

Larry paused and then explained Sam's presence to the woman. By the time he had finished the attention of everyone on the bus was focused on Sam. There was a lot of mumbling and a few people looked distinctly nervous, including the woman chewing betel nut. She turned away from Sam.

"Well, that seems to have done it," Sam said.

"Done what?"

"Made everyone nervous. What did you tell them, anyway?"

"I told them you were Jeff's father, that you were a policeman."

"They all look guilty."

"They're afraid."

"Afraid of what?"

Larry frowned. “In this country you don't get involved with the affairs of the police if you can avoid it. They don't know that there is anything different about Canadian police.”

“I see, but you're about to get involved with the affairs of the police. Doesn't that worry you?”

“I'm a blind man, Mr. Watson. They won't see me as much of a threat. They won't see you as much of a threat, either. A man who is deaf being led by one who is blind? They'll probably find it very funny.”

“That may be to our advantage.”

“Maybe, but you need to understand something first.”

“What's that?”

“You must do nothing to change their minds about us being no threat to them. If you do, our way will be much more difficult. You must not challenge the status or authority of the police here. They will treat you well because you are Jeff's father, a fellow police officer, and a foreigner, but this is their country. You are here as a tourist. That's what it says on your visa, doesn't it?”

“Yes.”

“Then you have no authority to act as a police officer here. Remember that. You must be subtle in everything you do. That's why it isn't wise for you to say that you are here to investigate your son's murder. That's why I didn't say anything about that when I explained why you were here. That could be very threatening to them. As it is, we may already be too late.”

“What do you mean?”

“After I explained why you are here—leaving out the part about investigating the murder—I heard a man's voice say you were here to do just that. It could be guesswork on his part or something about your intentions may have already come down the grapevine.

"Great," Sam said looking out the window. The town of Banmi was visible in the distance.

CHAPTER FIFTEEN

The Abbott led Tanait, now dressed in a brand new orange robe, to a small freestanding structure behind the residence where most of the novice monks stayed. "*Phra Tanait*," he said addressing Tanait as a monk for the first time. "These are your quarters."

"But this is a *Kuti*,"said Tanait in disbelief. "I'm only starting my life in the *Sangha*. I thought a *Kuti* was only for senior monks?"

"That is normally the case, yes, but I am making an exception."

Tanait studied the Abbott for a few moments. He had to choose his words carefully. "Reverend Abbott," he said, "My father is a man of great influence. I have spent much of the last few years trying to avoid the attachments that come with his position..."

The Abbott waved his hand to silence Tanait. "It is true that Lup Law has given a great deal to the temple in anticipation of your arrival here. But this is not why I have separated you from the other young monks. They do not have your seriousness of purpose. You already understand more of the *Dhamma* than most of them ever will.

Tanait allowed a faint smile to creep onto his face.

The Abbott caught this immediately. "But do not become proud. It is one thing to have a basic understanding of the teachings and quite another to put them into practice. This location will help you with the practical aspects of the path you have chosen."

Tanait nodded slowly.

"Remember," said the Abbott, "if the expectation is higher, so also is the risk of failure."

* * *

"He's going to Hua Hin."

Lup Law looked at the officer in front of him incredulously. "Hua Hin?"

"Yes."

"Why?"

"He went to your daughter's house. There was a post card there stuck on one of the beams along with a bunch of family photographs. The post card had a message on it from one of Ute's friends. It was an invitation from the friend to come and visit."

"Sticking to one of the beams in my daughter's house?"

"Yes."

Lup Law directed his attention to Kwanchai. "Why didn't we find that?"

"I don't know, Sir."

Lup Law shook his head. "A drunken third-rate hit man...Well, perhaps there is more to him than I thought." Lup Law looked at the officer again. "Go and take two others with you, and don't let him out of your sight."

The officer bowed and then left. Lup Law leaned forward and spoke softly to Kwanchai. "Any word on my daughter?"

"Nothing, Sir."

"Did you arrange to have the foreign exchange places watched?"

Kwanchai fidgeted and then spoke in a faltering voice. "They said that there were too many places to watch...and that you had run out of favors."

Lup Law regarded his lieutenant coolly for a moment. "Who told you I had run out of favors?"

Kwanchai swallowed. "Samrit," he said.

"In Bangkok?"

"Yes. And Thonburi didn't say that but they did say they didn't have the manpower ..."

Lup Law smiled grimly. "Maybe she's in Hua Hin."

"Do you really think she's trying to find him, Sir?"

"No. But then she did marry him, didn't she?"

Kwanchai did not respond to this.

Lup Law looked out his window at the reservoir, then at the tangle of trees that hid the river beyond it. He spoke softly. "Forget her. She has made her choice."

Kwanchai nodded slowly. "And what about Ute?"

Lup Law turned and looked at Kwanchai squarely. "What about him?"

* * *

The bus came to a stop in an empty parking lot ringed with open-air restaurants and little stalls that sold food and reading material. Everyone moved slowly, wilting in the heat. Sam watched most of the people get off the bus. "I guess we're here."

"Then we'd better get off," Larry replied.

"Yeah." Sam stood up and gave Larry his arm.

"You seem to be losing your enthusiasm."

"I'm just thinking, that's all." Sam led Larry down the aisle and off the bus.

"Now what?" Larry asked as the two stood in the sun

beside the bus.

"We find the police station. We ask questions."

"Could we find something to drink first?"

"Yeah, sure. Good idea." Sam surveyed the restaurants until he found one that had a cooler. He led Larry in that direction. They ordered two Pepsis from an athletic young man with a brush cut.

"*Pay nay khrap*?" The man said.

"What did he say?" Sam asked Larry.

"He wants to know where you're going."

"Why does everyone want to know where I'm going?"

"It's the standard greeting here. It's like 'how are you' in English."

"Oh. Well, what do you say back?"

"You tell him you're going to do business, or going on an outing. No one expects you to be specific."

"How do I say I'm going to do business?"

"*Pay tura*."

"*Pay tura*?"

"Yes."

"*Pay tura*," Sam said to the man.

The man nodded and smiled. He spoke to Larry. "*Ben tamruat, chai mai*?"

"*Chi*."

"Now what did he say?" Sam asked.

"He wanted confirmation that you were a police officer."

"And you gave it to him?"

"I think everyone knows."

Sam thought about this for a moment.

"When we ask where the police station is, that will confirm it anyway," Larry continued.

"But how did they find out? I've never been here

before except for that drive-through with Haddon, and we never spoke to anyone."

"But you did tell people in the church at Khoksamrong. A lot of people travel between here and Khoksamrong." Larry smiled and drank from his Pepsi.

"So now everybody will be intimidated when I talk to them."

"They would have been intimidated, anyway. There aren't many foreigners who come up here." Larry grinned. "Especially Canadian-born Chinese with names like Watson."

"Touché," Sam mumbled. He finished his drink. "So what should I do?"

"Do? It's more a matter of what you shouldn't do. Don't be aggressive. Don't push. Be friendly and patient."

Sam mulled this over. "How patient?"

"Only a Westerner would ask that question."

* * *

When Chiang handed the three American twenties to the bank teller in Thonburi, the first thing the woman did was to hold them up to the light and then flick them with her fingers.

"Is there a problem?" Chiang asked.

"No," said the woman, "They're all right. There are many counterfeits floating around these days. We've been told to watch out for them."

"I don't think there should be a problem," Chiang said thinking it unlikely that anyone would slip her father bogus cash.

"You never know."

Chiang could feel the woman's eyes studying her. Chiang was now wearing casual clothes, the kind of thing a factory worker might wear. She did this to blend in, to be inconspicuous. But she forgot about one thing. One would not normally expect a factory worker to go to the foreign exchange wicket with sixty American dollars. That was more than a month's wages and in a foreign currency. The teller was right to be suspicious.

"No, I suppose not," Chiang said.

The woman began counting out hundred *baht* notes. "Get it from your boy friend?" she asked casually.

"He didn't have any Thai money left," Chiang said, glad of the assumption.

"Be careful," the teller said, sliding the money through the hole in the glass. "Some of them have sickness."

"Sickness?"

"It's a very bad sickness that you get through sex. People who get it all eventually die." The woman grinned. "Make him wear a *Meechai*."

Chiang smiled and looked suitably embarrassed. A *Meechai* was a condom, named after a popular Thai social activist who had advocated its use in the late sixties and early seventies as a means of birth control. Chiang thanked the teller and slipped the money into her bra. She walked back down the street to the place where she had seen a clothing store and went inside.

Fifteen minutes later she emerged with her factory clothes now in her bag and wearing a suit, the style of which was common to office girls and bank tellers in Bangkok. It was also dressy enough to allow her to enter the good tourist hotels without attracting attention.

* * *

"Ask him what his name is."

The tattooed pedicab driver was in the process of hopping onto his seat after doing a little running push to get the vehicle going. He settled into a slow but steady pace almost immediately.

"Why do you want to know that?" Larry asked, his body pressed tightly into his half of the tiny passenger seat. "This man is not important to you."

"Just being friendly. You said to be friendly, didn't you?"

Larry asked the man's name.

"Bua Tong," came the reply. The man turned and gave Sam a brief chipped toothed smile.

Sam caught the scent of cheap whiskey. He smiled at the man and then spoke to Larry. "If he was in Canada, I'd bust him for impaired driving."

"Not a very friendly thing to do."

"Ask him how long he's lived here."

"About ten years. He's originally from Lamnurai," came the reply.

"Where's that?"

"It's on the other side of Khoksamrong, I think. I'm not really sure, but I know people from there who sometimes came to the church in Khoksamrong.

"Ask him about his family."

The reply this time was much longer with Larry interjecting several times before speaking to Sam. "His wife and two sons live in the Lamnurai area. He hasn't seen them in five or six years. He says he had another son by a woman who lives in Lopburi. She left the baby in the hospital and it was sent to an orphanage.

"They left the child in the hospital?"

"Yes."

"Just left it?"

"Yes."

Sam thought about this for a moment and then decided he didn't want to ask any more questions.

Bua Tong pulled the pedicab up in front of the police station, which, it turned out, was only a few blocks from where the bus had stopped. He helped Larry and Sam out of the vehicle. Sam pulled two twenty-*baht* notes out of his wallet and handed it to the man for a ten-*baht* fare. He waved off the change knowing that the man would spend the money on whiskey. Perhaps he would think of his abandoned son as he drank.

* * *

The man at the hotel desk was amused. "This is a tourist hotel, Madam." he said. "Only the richest Thais stay here."

"I'd like to stay for two nights," Chiang said. "Until my flight leaves."

"Oh, and where are you going?" the man asked.

"Germany."

"All right," said the man without moving. "And how would you like to pay for that?"

Chiang reached into her bosom and pulled out her roll of American money. "In cash, of course" she said counting out four twenty-dollar bills.

The man's eyes widened. "Yes... yes of course," He stammered. "I'm afraid we have nothing on the higher floors. Would you like the second, third, or fourth? All have a view of the river."

Chiang couldn't understand what was so special about the river. It was brown, dirty, and frequently had mounds of floating garbage. Why would anybody want to view that? Perhaps it was the boats that the foreigners found interesting. "The fourth," she said.

The man looked at the bag at Chiang's feet. "Will there be any other luggage?" he asked.

"I'm traveling light," she said.

The man nodded and handed Chiang the room key. "Take the elevator to the fourth floor. The room will be to your left when you get off. I'm afraid we don't leave the air conditioners on when the rooms are unoccupied. It will take a few minutes for the room to get comfortable." He gestured to a room across the lobby from the reception desk. "May I suggest that you cool off in our lounge while you're waiting?"

Chiang looked through the door into the room beyond. A number of people were milling about, mostly white and middle-aged or older. She smiled back at the man. "Perhaps I will," she said. She picked up her bag and went to the elevator.

Alone in the elevator, her heart beat rapidly and her face began to flush. She took several deep breaths trying to recompose herself during the elevator's short trip to the fourth floor. When the doors opened there was no one in sight. The door to her room was only a few paces from the elevator. She put the key in the lock and entered quickly, almost slamming the door behind her.

Inside, the room was stuffy and dim. She found the air conditioner control and turned it on. There was an instant blast of cool air from somewhere in front of her. She found the light switch and turned it on. She was greeted by teak furniture consisting of a small chest of drawers, a writing desk and a queen sized quilted bed with a headboard, and two night tables. On one of these was a remote control for a Sanyo TV, which sat on a rolling stand in the corner.

Chiang pushed at the bed's mattress and found it firm. She dropped the bag on it and then retraced her steps to the door, finding the entrance to the bathroom in the process. She went in and looked at herself in the mirror. There was a hint of panic in the eyes, but otherwise things looked good. She took out the American money and counted it. She had spent well over a hundred dollars in less than twenty-four hours. She would have to work fast.

* * *

A group of cigarette-smoking policemen stood under a shelter and watched as Sam led Larry slowly up the sidewalk to the police station. He heard muted laughter and bits of conversation. "Can you hear what they're saying?" he asked Larry.

"Who?"

"There's a group of officers watching us."

Larry listened for a moment before replying. "Well, they know who you are, that's for sure. And they think it's pretty funny that you're here with me."

Sam pursed his lips but said nothing. He looked at the building in front of him. It was older than most of the other government buildings he'd seen in the area and was made primarily of wood. This had been either painted or stained green—he wasn't sure which—but for all its apparent age the building was in good repair. The eaves and accents had the same simple flare he'd seen in other Thai wooden buildings but there was nothing particularly ornate about it. It was government-functional but warmer than the other buildings.

"You're lucky," Larry said. "Captain Lup Law is here. Apparently he's been out quite a bit lately."

Sam looked over at the men under the shelter. From this distance, he could barely hear their speech. "You have better ears than I have."

"Better-tuned."

Sam helped Larry up the six steps to the entrance. The door was open. Inside, to their immediate left, were bars. Behind these, a small boy cowered on a bench. Sam guessed his age to be eight, maybe nine.

Larry felt Sam stiffen. "What?" he asked.

"They have a kid in the cell."

"A kid?"

"There's a cell to the left of us. There's a boy in it. Can't be more than ten but he looks younger. He also looks very scared."

"Anyone else around?"

To their right a police officer behind a desk was regarding them quizzically. "There's an officer to your right."

Larry spoke to the man for a few moments and then turned to Sam. "As I said before, the captain is in. He's expecting you upstairs."

"What about the kid?"

"What about him?"

"Well, why is he in there?"

"I don't know, but the captain is waiting to see us."

"Just ask, okay?"

Larry asked the officer who seemed amused by Sam's interest.

“He was caught stealing things from people on the train,” Larry said. “It happened between Lopburi and here so they took him into custody when the train stopped. They don't know where he's from. He won't talk.”

“How long have they had him?”

Larry spoke to the man again. “About two days,” came the reply.

“He's been in that cell for two days?”

“I guess so.”

“What will they do with him?”

“Wait until he talks, I guess. We should go and see the captain now.”

The child was now regarding Sam expectantly. The officer behind the desk spoke to him and then laughed. The child turned away.

“What was that all about?” Sam asked Larry.

“He said you were an American cop and that American cops knew how to loosen the tongues of small boys.”

“Great.”

“We should go.”

“I’m concerned about the boy.”

“We’re here to talk to Captain Lup Law. The boy is not your concern,” Larry said.

Sam led Larry up the stairs; at the top was a hallway with several doors. One of these was open and the man inside gestured to Sam and pointed down the hallway with his pen. Sam nodded to the man and led Larry down the hall not knowing where, precisely, they should stop. The answer came in the form of a door with the words “Police Captain” printed in English. Sam knocked.

The door opened and a thirtyish man in a brush cut

bowed to them and then gestured palm to floor for them to enter. He retreated to a corner of the room. Another man, this one balding and heavy-set with two scars on his right cheek, sat behind a large teak desk. He had his fingers around an amulet that hung from his neck. This he released, then he stood up and walked around the end of his desk.

"Welcome, Jep's father," he said, smiling and extending his hand.

Sam took the hand and shook it firmly. "You are the police captain?"

"Captain Lup Law, yes."

"You speak English?"

"English? No. Little bit." The captain gestured to Larry. "But you have blind man," he said and smiled.

Sam looked at Larry and saw no reaction. He turned back to the captain. "Larry is my translator, yes."

Lup Law continued to smile. There was a short silence and then the captain gestured to the officer with the brush cut. The man left the room. Lup Law spoke rapidly to Larry.

"He said that the lieutenant will get us something to drink. In the meantime, he wants to know how he can help you." Larry switched into a deep Southern drawl. "Remember, you are not a police officer here. You are a tourist."

Sam nodded and then realized the gesture was useless. "Tell him I am very grieved at the loss of my only son and want to know if they've caught his killer yet."

Lup Law's countenance became serious as he listened to Larry. At length Larry gave the reply.

"He is upset by your son's case because he regarded

your son as a friend and was deeply saddened by his death. That his own son-in-law was involved made things much more difficult, not because he loves his son-in-law, but because he loves his daughter. His daughter made a serious mistake getting involved with him. The son-in-law is an ex-police officer who was corrupt and had to be fired. This, as it turned out, was a complicating factor because, as an ex-police officer, his son-in-law knew police procedures and this helped him to evade capture."

"Ask him why his son-in-law would want to murder Jeff."

Lup Law looked uncomfortable with the question.

"He may have been hired to kill Jeff or he may have done it out of jealousy. The Captain's daughter, Chiang, is very beautiful and so there's a possibility that Jeff may have been attracted to her. They also lived close to each other. Many of the neighbours said that they saw the two of them together. This is what the newspapers like to write about, so jealousy is the most popular theory."

"Ask him if there are other reasons why he suspects his son-in-law."

"He says that the man who shot Jeff was riding a brand-new Kawasaki water-cooled motorcycle. It was a new model and very expensive. There were only a few on the road at the time of Jeff's murder and his son-in-law owned one of them. That, in itself, was suspicious because the son-in-law had no money to buy such a machine and claimed that he won it in a lottery. The police have checked all the local lotteries and none of them had such a prize."

"So he thinks his son-in-law was hired to kill my son and that the bike was payment?"

Lup Law nodded to this suggestion.

"Ask him how the investigation is going."

"He said that for a while things were going quite slowly, but they now have a strategy. His daughter ran away from home a short while ago. She has little sense and is quite protective of her husband, despite his abuse. Anyway, his officers are following his daughter in Bangkok, and Captain Lup Law believes that she will soon lead them to his son-in-law."

The lieutenant then shuffled into the room carrying a tray with three bottles of Singha beer on it. The captain offered these to Sam and Larry.

"He wants to know if you've ever tried Thai beer," Larry said. "He says that most Westerners find it refreshing."

Sam watched as the captain took a bottle and poured him a glass. "Thank you," he said as he took the glass. After taking a sip he said it was very good. The look on Larry's face told Sam that this made him quite uncomfortable. "You have a problem with this?"

"I don't drink alcohol."

"Then tell him so," Sam said.

"I thought police officers in Canada didn't drink when they were working."

"I'm not working. I'm a tourist, remember?"

Larry said nothing.

Sam smiled and then spoke rapidly. "Larry, I'm going to socialize for a short while with this man and then we're going to leave. I want to make sure that we leave on good terms. In the meantime, you just tell him that your condition does not allow for the consumption of alcoholic beverages."

"That is not why I don't drink."

"Then tell him what you like but make sure it leaves a good impression."

Larry said something to the captain that seemed to have the desired results. Lup Law nodded and then touched glasses with Sam.

CHAPTER SIXTEEN

Bom was now continuously ill. He had developed strange skin rashes, now had a perpetually stuffed-up nose and his cough was much worse. Then he got pneumonia, his eyesight began to fail, his lymph nodes started to swell, and he had frequent bouts of diarrhea. He'd lost weight, a lot of weight, so much so that Ute had no trouble lifting him into the pedicab for the trip to the hospital.

Bom hadn't wanted to go to the hospital. "It's a place where people die," he said.

"It's a place where people get well," Ute argued but he had to admit his own experience was like Bom's. As a cop, he'd had occasion to take a few people to the hospital, road-accident people. Motorcyclists mostly. Only one had made it. That man now sat at the back of his parent's restaurant and grinned stupidly at people. Ute's own father had died in a hospital, unable to get his breath. You only went to hospital if you were seriously ill, if the five-*baht* drugs they gave you at the drug store didn't work. That was the common wisdom. But Ute knew the hospitals these days were a lot better than they were twenty years ago. They had Western-trained doctors now, or at least doctors trained in Western medicine. Going there was no longer a death sentence.

"I don't have anybody to look after me," Bom said.

This was true. Bom had no relatives, no one to stay with him in the hospital and take care of his needs. For a while, Ute accepted this as a good argument. But as Bom got worse, Ute realized that he was spending all his time looking after his friend anyway. What difference did the location make? "I'll take care of you," he said feeling strange at his own willingness to go that far for somebody.

They had been in the hospital now for nearly a week. The doctor had taken a blood sample and sent it to Bangkok for analysis. He had also asked a lot of questions about Bom's sexual preferences. The doctor was cheerful and encouraging and the drugs he gave, while not exactly curing the problem, were at least making Bom's breathing easier and reducing his pain.

Ute took a long pull on his cigarette and blew the smoke out the window by Bom's bed. You weren't supposed to smoke on the ward, but no one challenged him. He heard footsteps behind him and turned. He found the doctor looking glumly down on the sleeping Bom. He held up a yellow piece of paper and beckoned for Ute to follow.

In the office, the doctor laid the paper before him on the table and gave a phony smile. "You can take him home tomorrow," he said.

"But, he's very ill..."

"I'll give you a supply of the necessary drugs. They can be administered there just as easily as they can here." He smiled again. "He'll be able to go home and we'll have the hospital bed for someone else."

Ute looked at the doctor. "What has he got?"

The doctor stood up, scooped up the paper, and stuffed it into the pocket of his lab coat. "Just give him the drugs and he'll be fine," he said and began walking to the door.

Ute barred his way. "I said, what has he got?"

“If you just give him the drugs, then—”

Ute grabbed the doctor by the collar of his coat and lifted him six inches off the ground. “Tell me!”

“Cool your heart, my friend, cool your heart!”

Ute lowered the doctor to the ground and released him, but he continued to bar his way.

“AIDS,” the doctor said quietly, straightening his collar. “And he's quite far along. So you see all we can do is keep him comfortable. Give him lots of drugs to kill the pain. There's no reason why you can't do that at home.”

“The gay disease?”

“Well, they think it was brought into the country by gay men from the West, yes.”

“And you get it from sex?”

“That and dirty needles, if you're a drug user, that is.”

“Sex,” Ute repeated. He and Bom had shared many partners.

* * *

One look at the drink prices in the hotel lounge convinced Chiang that it was not the place where she wanted to begin her quest. Besides, the men in the hotel lounge were too old. Instead, she found a bar a short walk from the hotel where the drinks were cheaper and the men younger.

Most of the women in the bar were dressed provocatively, tight jeans, short shorts, or mini-skirts with wispy T-shirts or see-through blouses. It was not a game that Chiang had played before, and her office suit was clearly out of place. Still, she was more attractive than most of the women and she was noticed.

Chiang sat down on a bar stool, ordered a whiskey, and crossed her legs, allowing the skirt to hike its way up. She could feel the resentment of the women and the burning eyes of the pimps who smoked at a table in the corner. She paid for the whiskey, using an American fifty.

It took only about ten minutes for a man to sit beside her and lightly touch her arm. He was Caucasian with light brown hair and gray eyes, and looked to be in his early thirties. He was not a handsome man but he had a good body and wore better clothes than most of the bar's clients.

"Do you come here often?" he said in Thai.

"You speak Thai?" Chiang said in surprise.

"I come here often." The man laughed. "Every year for two or three months. I've been doing that for ten years now. I love your country, so I've made an effort to learn the language."

"You speak it very well."

"Thank you."

"Where are you from?"

"I'm Dutch, actually, but I work on the oil platforms in the North Sea. It's good money. What about you? What do you do?"

Chiang was not expecting this question and had not prepared an answer. "I, uh...I'm a model," she said.

The man spoke softly. "You know, of course, that the girls who work this bar are not happy you're here. Neither are the fellows who watch over them. Only that stunt with the American fifty kept them from coming over here for a talk. They're expecting someone else to show up, so if no one does you could be in for a rough evening."

"What makes you think I don't have someone coming?"

The man smiled warmly. "I've been coming here for ten years. You've got all the wrong moves. You're out of your element."

Chiang studied her glass and said nothing.

"You're also too good for this place. Finish your drink and I'll take you someplace much better." He gestured to the dancers on their little platforms behind the bar. "A place where you won't have to deal with this."

"I don't know your name."

The man shrugged. "And I don't know yours."

Someplace much better turned out to be the hotel lounge.

* * *

Sam stood in front of the sink and washed his own shirt and then Larry's. It was a trick he'd learned from Janet. She told him if he wanted to travel light in a tropical country, then the thing to do was to take only a few shirts, wash them every night in the hotel room, and hang them up. They would be dry by mid-morning of the next day. He hadn't counted on washing Larry's shirts, but who else was going to do it?

"You have a servant's heart," Larry told him as he lay on his bed, head strapped into his headphones.

"Will you take that thing off! I want to talk to you."

"What?"

"I said take the headphones off so I can talk to you!"

"Oh, sorry," Larry said, removing the headphones.

"The best thing, of course, would be to find this son-in-law before they do. But that seems unlikely given that they have all the resources and it's their country. At least the captain was kind enough to give me the man's picture." Sam laughed. "Maybe we'll get lucky and spot him in a crowd."

"I won't spot him."

"No I don't suppose you will."

"His name is Ute, by the way. That's his nickname any way."

"Nickname?"

"Yes. Most Thais go by nick names, not their real names. It means camel. Does he look like a camel?"

Sam wiped his hands off and walked over to the desk to look at the picture. "No," he said. "You know, I must be slipping. It never even occurred to me to ask his name. I guess I just thought it was something cultural about having the guy constantly being referred to as son-in-law. Must be because I'm over sixty."

"Over sixty?"

"Never mind." Sam studied the picture for a moment, trying to memorize the features. He wasn't at all sure he would recognize the man even if he saw him. He looked like everyone else until one got past his "Thainess." Would he have time to do that in a brief encounter, assuming one even had a brief encounter, which he thought unlikely?

"So what do we do now?" Larry asked.

"I guess go back to Bangkok. Maybe try following the police who are following the daughter. I don't know."

"You don't want to go and interview the villagers?"

"I don't think that would accomplish anything. For one thing, the basic facts are pretty well established. The only thing to try to find out is whether anyone local had a reason to get rid of him. A gem merchant, perhaps?

Jeff was concerned about the way they treated their employees. Maybe he rubbed somebody the wrong way. If it was a contract killing, that seems like the best motive to me. The thing is how do I do that without acting like a cop? And if the cops were in on it, it could be dangerous."

"That is a very wise if," Larry said, "but I don't think you should go to Bangkok because one cannot follow the police dragging a blind man, certainly not inconspicuously. Besides, I don't think anything is actually happening there."

"You don't think the police are following his daughter?"

"Well, do you think the captain was a personal friend of your son's?"

"No."

"And do you think that Ute was let go from the police force because of corruption?"

"Doesn't make much sense, does it?"

"I think maybe we should go to the beach," Larry said.

"The beach?"

"Have a holiday."

"What?"

"A lot of people think that, because a blind man does not look at them while they are talking, that he is, therefore, not listening."

"What did you hear?"

"Three officers are going to Hua Hin. I'm not sure why, but it has something to do with this case."

"Where is Hua Hin?"

"It's a beach resort a few hours south of Bangkok."

"Then Ute may be there?"

"And you have a picture and Hua Hin is much smaller

than Bangkok."

* * *

Two of the three police officers on the train with Nak were asleep. The other regarded him shrewdly over the top of a hand of cards. All three thought of this assignment as something of a lark. Help the real assassin find the false assassin and bring him in to stand trial. Lup Law must have bananas for brains, they said. The man would make a break for it at his first opportunity. But they would be ready and they were armed.

* * *

The Dutch man was now buying the drinks. They were expensive, but he didn't seem to care and Chiang was beginning to feel a bit out of control. So far, however, she had managed to keep him talking about himself and his home in Groningen in the north of Holland.

"It's an apartment," he said, "but a large one, over a thousand square meters. And it has all the best appliances, multi-channel TV with cable, a stereo VCR that plugs right into a digital home theatre system...Right now the apartment is just an investment. I might spend a grand total of two months a year there. My sister keeps the place now, but she's hunting for an apartment of her own and should be out by the time I get back. Then I suppose I'll have to find someone else to stay there." He laughed. "Either that or find a job locally and settle down."

"Are there lots of jobs there?" Chiang asked.

"For a person with my skills, yeah. I'm both a

qualified welder and machinist. It's a good combination." The Dutch man lit a cigarette and let his eyes roam over her body, not trying to hide his interest. "And what about you? I've been practicing my Thai all night."

"My life is not very interesting."

"But you're a model. I would think that would be glamorous."

Chiang was beginning to feel warm. She liked the way the chest hair filled the "v" in the Dutch man's shirt. She liked the way the biceps moved beneath the tattooed skin of his arm. "I put clothes on and take them off and put clothes on again. People take pictures," she said with a shrug and a grin.

"And what part of town do you live in?"

"I live here," Chiang said.

"Here?"

"Yes, here in this hotel."

* * *

The patriarch paid few visits to other people. Most came to him, wanting the favors that only his kind of power could grant. He was the one person in Banmi that Lup Law feared and he had just walked into Lup Law's office unannounced.

"Some of my employees are talking," the old man said. "They say the man I hired has been drunk and has talked about what he did. They say many people in town know and now we have an American cop here, wanting to know who killed his son."

"He's Canadian," Lup Law said.

The patriarch waved this off. "It may get back to me. I

don't want this kind of trouble when I'm preparing to die. It's not how I want to end my life. You and I had a deal. I've done what I agreed to do and paid what I've agreed to pay. Now you must do what you've agreed to do, arrest your son-in-law."

Lup Law smiled and involuntarily clutched the amulet around his neck. "Ute is in Hua Hin." "I've just sent three officers to get him."

"Yes, and you've also sent the killer himself, did you not? And you told him that, if he didn't get your son-in-law, he would have to pay for the crime after all. Where would that leave me, assuming that happened? Disgraced in my death! How could you possibly convict him without dragging me into it? And then, of course, there's the matter of the money I paid to make sure he wasn't convicted. Or have you forgotten about that?"

"I haven't forgotten. I assure you this is just a ploy to ensure Ute's arrest. My men will not allow a third-rate hit man to..."

"That third-rate hit man took three minutes to find an important lead that your 'officers' somehow missed and he did it in a state of intoxication. I'll grant that he's not overly bright, but what does that say about your officers? No. This is not acceptable. I want you there. I want you to arrest your son-in-law."

"Me?"

"Yes."

The patriarch did not wait for a response. He turned and walked out the door, leaving Lup Law to finger his amulet.

* * *

The Dutch man's hand rested on Chiang's hip as she inserted her key into the hotel room door. He had a slightly musky, sweaty smell in spite of sitting in an air-conditioned lounge for more than two hours. Chiang's friends had told her that Western men sweat too much and often smell bad, but Chiang found the smell exciting. It was the alcohol talking, she knew, but she wanted it to talk.

The door swung open and Chiang stepped back to allow the Dutch man to enter. He walked in, casually looked around, and smiled. The door clicked shut behind Chiang.

"You live here," the Dutch man said, nodding. It was a statement and not a question. He pulled off his shirt, rolled it into a ball, and tossed it onto the chair in the corner. His back was to Chiang as he flexed his muscles. He turned slowly to face Chiang. "You live here, but you have not lived here long. Perhaps a few hours?"

Chiang started to back up but the Dutch man caught her and, as he began tearing at her clothing, she realized that he did smell bad.

* * *

The express train did not stop in Banmi, but it did in Lopburi. Lup Law looked at his watch and gave the BMW a little more gas. There was a place near the Lopburi train station where he could leave his car. He had thought briefly of taking the vehicle all the way to Hua Hin, but the long drive would leave him tired and he didn't like the idea of using the car for police work. Something could happen to it. The express train would be faster and he would arrive rested, ready to deal with the situation. It was also likely he would catch up with his men, who had left with Nak an hour earlier aboard a regular train.

Lup Law's friend owned an automotive shop about five minutes from the train station. He pulled the BMW up to the front of the building and honked his horn.

His friend emerged wiping oil from his hands and grinned at Lup Law. "Surely you're not having a problem with all that German technology?" he said.

"It runs fine, but it could stop a bit better. About time for an oil change too." He got out of the car and threw his friend the keys. "I'll be in Bangkok for a couple of days. I'll pick it up on the way back."

"Sure," said the friend, looking at his watch. "Are you trying to catch the express? If you are, you've got about five minutes."

Lup Law didn't answer, but reached into his back seat and pulled out his bag.

"See you in a couple of days, then," the friend said, shaking his head as Lup Law ran for the train.

Lup Law was panting as he came up to the ticket counter and asked for first-class passage on the train. It was a new experience because, when in uniform, he always rode for free.

"First-class?" The ticket clerk said. "I'm sorry Sir, but you can only buy first-class tickets at the train's point of origin. I'll sell you a second-class and you can upgrade on the train if there are any seats left in the first-class car."

Lup Law could see the train pulling into the station. "Yes, that would be fine, but please hurry."

The man handed Lup Law the ticket and the captain

began making his way to the train. He ran up to the first-class car but then came to an abrupt halt. There, in front of him and climbing into the car, was the Canadian cop and his blind interpreter.

Lup Law looked quickly for the second-class car.

CHAPTER SEVENTEEN

There would be a wait at the Samsen station in Bangkok, two and a half hours, the wicket clerk in Banmi had said. Nak looked at his watch, a gold Rolex copy that lost about six minutes a day. Two of those hours were gone. He had less than half an hour before the southern express would arrive to take them to Hua Hin, unless he was successful at ditching his three companions.

Two of them sat on either side of him on the bench and the third paced and smoked in front of them. The captain had told them that if they lost him they would lose more than that. Lup Law had spoken the words in Nak's hearing to let him know that the men would be highly motivated. What they would lose was unclear but Nak could see that his companions took the threat seriously.

He had expected them to keep close and to keep him in sight at all times, but they were practically on top of him. They knew as well as he did that losing sight of him in Bangkok would mean losing sight of him permanently. Bangkok was his best chance of escape and they all knew it. He had one chance, and that chance would be arriving in twenty-five minutes.

* * *

Chiang stood in the shower and let warm water wash over her again and again. The small bar of soap that had come with the room was now gone, washed down the drain in countless lathers. The Dutch man was also gone. He had taken her quickly and then pocketed the American money he found lying on the floor with Chiang's torn clothing.

* * *

Sam watched out the window as the train pulled out of the Don Muang station. Larry had told him that he would have to watch for Samsen, the station where they would make the transfer to the southbound train. His companion wasn't sure exactly where this station was, only that it was past the airport station.

Then Larry laughed.

"What?" Sam said.

Larry grinned. "I was just thinking that this is like Heaven. It's air-conditioned, the seats are so comfortable, they feed us wonderful food, bring us drinks, and serve us continually. That is how I think Heaven will be but, of course, we will also constantly worship God while we are eating and drinking wonderful food and I will be able to see and there will be wonderful jazz and gospel music..." He laughed again. "You see, this little taste of Heaven has come to me through you and you're not even a believer!"

Sam studied Larry for a moment. "Perhaps, then, it's not a taste of Heaven. Perhaps it's something very evil made to seem like Heaven."

Larry thought about this for a moment. "No," he said. "I will receive it as a gift from God and be grateful."

Sam shook his head. "This is not God's doing. This is me spending more money than I should because I can't bear the heat any longer."

"That may be, but I think you are God's instrument sent to give me a blessing."

Sam smiled. "Well, I've been called many things in my time but this is the first time anyone has ever called me God's instrument."

"You don't have to be a believer to be an instrument of God. The Bible is full of stories of people God used to bring about his will, even though they were opposed to him. God can use whomever he wants."

"And how exactly do you know I'm not a believer?"

"You don't act like a believer."

"How's that?"

Larry said nothing.

"You're benefiting from this little obsession of mine, you know," Sam said.

Again, Larry said nothing.

"What am I supposed to do?" Sam said angrily. "Turn the other cheek? Maybe bring my daughter over here and offer her to the killer?"

Larry sat on his hands and pursed his lips. After a few moments, his mouth began moving silently.

Great, now he's praying for me. Sam looked out the window and saw a sign that told him Samsen was the next station.

"Come on, Larry. Samsen is the next stop."

"Well, are you?"

"Am I what?"

"A believer."

Sam looked at Larry, stood up, and began gathering the baggage. "I know the basic teachings of Christianity because they were spoon fed to me as a kid and I know more about the Bible than most people because my wife was obsessed with it, but I'm not what you would call a believer, no."

Lup Law stood at the door of the train as it pulled into Samsen station. He wanted to be across the platform and out of sight before his men and their charge noticed him. That way he could work quickly once he hit Hua Hin, without having to drag the other four around.

As the train slowed down he saw his men in a tight group around Nak at the north end of the platform. They were talking, smoking, and paying little attention to the train pulling into the station. Why should they? The train was not the one they were waiting for and they weren't expecting him to be on it. His car was near the front of the train, so he would disembark at the south end. It should be a simple matter to walk across the platform and disappear among the food stalls.

The train stopped and Lup Law got off and walked quickly across the platform and into the deep shade of an open-air noodle shop. He sat down and looked in the direction of his men. They showed no sign of having seen him. He smiled, began ordering a Coke, and stopped in the middle of the request.

There, standing on the platform and helping his blind friend disembark, was the Canadian cop. There was no reason for them to be getting off here other than to change to a southbound train. Somehow, they knew of the possibility of finding Ute in Hua Hin.

It was now only ten minutes before the southbound train was scheduled to arrive, ten minutes until Nak would make his break. If they got on this train in the same manner that they got on the one in Banmi, he had a reasonable chance. It would be a matter of timing.

“Well, look at that will you?” said one of his escorts, gesturing to the other end of the platform.

“What?” said one of his partners.

“Isn't that the American cop?”

Nak looked down the platform. A heavy set, balding Westerner dressed in a Hawaiian floral-print shirt appeared to be helping a Thai man to walk. It took a moment before Nak realized that the man was blind.

“Yes, that's him,” said the third cop. “He's Canadian, actually, though I don't see that it makes much difference. I wonder what he's doing here.”

“It's obvious to me,” said the first.

The three men looked at each other.

“Not bad for someone who doesn't know the language,” said the second.

“Well, we'll know for sure if they get on the train.”

Good, thought Nak. Something to distract them. He took a long look at the father of the man he had killed.

“*Khop khun khrap*,” Larry said to the woman on the platform. He turned to Sam. “The southbound express is scheduled to be here in about seven minutes.”

Sam nodded and then checked himself. “Good, looks like we'll make the connection.”

Nak watched the southbound express approach the station. The fingers of his left hand told him the contents of his pocket; a few hundred *baht*, an old imitation Swiss army knife and his train ticket. These things and his life would be all he had left if he was successful. And if he failed? He could only hope it was fatal and not a failure for which he'd spent the rest of his life in prison.

As the train pulled into the station, he stood up and lifted the old army duffel he used as a travel bag. He turned and looked at his three companions.

"Looks like we made our connection," he said weakly.

"You get on first, and remember we're right behind you," said the first cop.

About fifteen people pushed up to the stairs leading into the coach. Nak joined this group and felt the soft stomach of the first cop push into his back. The other two cops crammed in behind the first cop and several other people pushed behind them.

Nak waited until he reached the top of the stairs and then threw his elbow hard into the solar plexus of the cop behind him. The man gasped and, as he fell backward, Nak threw the army duffel on top of him. Nak then bolted out the door on the other side of the train. To his right a crowd of people had just disembarked. He veered immediately to his left, staying low beneath the windows and as close to the cars as possible. When he had run two coach lengths he jumped back onto the train, glancing back to see all three policemen emerge two cars back with their guns drawn. They plunged immediately into the crowd and fanned out through it, none of them looking his direction.

Nak watched as they pushed through the people and ran toward the concession carts on that platform. None of them looked back at the train, which, by then, was starting to pull away from the station. Nak smiled, took a deep breath, and nonchalantly made his way to one of the few unoccupied seats.

Only one elderly man seemed to be paying any attention to him. Nak tried to ignore the man, but soon caught his eye. The man gave him a gummy smile and a victory sign.

Lup Law heard only a few muffled shouts and saw nothing. He was about to write it off as a minor disturbance when he saw movement outside his window. His three men were pushing through the crowd with their guns held high. Lup Law looked for Nak but could not see him. His men appeared equally uncertain about the location of their quarry. Lup Law felt the train move and saw his men pay no attention to this. As the train pulled away from the platform, he wondered in which car Nak was hiding.

"So, how long until we're in Hua Hin?" Sam asked Larry as the two settled in their first-class seats for the remainder of the journey.

"I'm not sure. Just ask one of the attendants," Larry said using his sense of touch to fit the new batteries Sam had purchased on the platform into his tape player.

"Ask them?"

"This is first-class, remember? First-class is for tourists."

Sam got the attention of one of the attendants who told him the trip would take about four hours. He looked at his watch. That would put them into Hua Hin around 10:00 p.m.

"You sure we'll be able to just walk into any hotel and get a room?" he asked Larry. "We're going to be getting in pretty late."

"It's off-season and it's not like Phataya or Pukhet. It's not a big resort yet. Until a few years ago, tourists didn't even know it existed." He laughed. "When I was with the travel agency, we used to send all the tourists there who wanted to get away from other tourists. Not now, though. It's supposed to be overdeveloped. There's been a lot of speculation and construction to the point where they have trouble filling the rooms even in peak season. We won't have any trouble."

"Good, then I think I'll try and get a little shut-eye. First class or not, riding all day on trains isn't my idea of Heaven."

The decision to get back on the train was a snap one. Nak had hoped to disappear into Bangkok's millions, but the distance between the train and the far end of the platform was too great. There was no place to hide in between unless one wanted to hide behind people. The crowd itself was both too thick to allow him to move swiftly and too thin to allow him to disappear. Getting back on the train was risky, but it had worked. He now had the luxury of time to work out his next move.

His first thought had been to get off the train at one of the other stops before it left the city's suburbs. That would still allow him to disappear, and it had the added advantage of not giving the police any idea about where he had actually entered the city.

The appearance of the Canadian cop had, however, given him a more interesting option. Lup Law's decision to put pressure on Nak in the first place was all to do with the captain's fear of losing face in front of this man. If he was eliminated, especially if it happened a long way from Lup Law's jurisdiction, then the pressure would be off. Nak smiled at the beauty of it.

His mission, Lup Law reminded himself, was to get Ute and bring him back to be tried and convicted of the Jep's murder. The assassin's escape and the loss of his men didn't change that. To go back through the train now until he found and arrested Nak would only complicate matters and delay the completion of his mission. At the very least he would have to get off the train, take Nak to some local detachment, turn him in, and then wait several hours to catch the next train south. As it was, Nak was likely to leave the train at first available opportunity and escape into the city.

The assassin was not important now. Nak had no more information about Ute's whereabouts than Lup Law had and his escape from Lup Law's men meant that it was extremely unlikely that he would ever be seen in Banmi again. There would, therefore, be little chance of his further embarrassing the patriarch.

Lup Law smiled at the irony of it. After all these years in the police force, he was finally going to get the chance to do some real detective work. He had no doubt that he would succeed, and he smiled at the thought of the prestige it would bring him.

For Nak, the only real problem was what to use for a weapon. His gun was several hundred kilometers away beneath a friend's floorboards. Retrieving it was out of the question. Knives and other such items were easy to get—he even had a small one in his pocket—but they required one to work at close quarters and had a tendency to be imprecise and messy. The Canadian cop was old, but he had probably been well trained. There was always the chance that he would survive such an attack and perhaps even fight back.

Nak smiled as these thoughts rolled through his head. Was he afraid of such an old man? No, it wasn't fear that made him hesitate. It was the possibility of imprecision, the thought that things might not go smoothly. A gun would be smooth and precise, but where to get one? And how much time did he have?

The smile on his face dissolved and then grew again. If there was one thing that he knew about trains, it was that they usually contained sleeping police officers sprawled across unpaid second-class seats with their guns strapped to their hips in full view of everyone. Why they always rode the train like this was never clear to Nak, but he suspected that they were doing it because they could. No one would dare ask to see their fare. It was arrogance, pure and simple, and with such arrogance often came an absence of caution. If Nak was careful and lucky—and luck was clearly with him on this day—he might well succeed in relieving one of these fellows of his weapon.

Sam opened his eyes. The countryside was darkening outside the train. Palm trees, mango trees...rice? Whatever it was growing in those fields made them greener than the ones around Banmi. He could see that, even in this twilight. And people. There were always people watching the train.

Nak stuck his head out the window and counted the number of cars to the front of the train. There were eight, three third, two second, and three first-class cars. The police would be in the second-class car closest to the front, the one adjacent the first-class section. They would want to be close to those who had money and were important.

He looked at his imitation Rolex. It had stopped. The

dial read 6:07. The time of my escape, thought Nak with a smile. He shook his wrist and watched as the second hand resumed its jerky movement. A fellow passenger's watch was illuminated, so he set his to it. Nearly three hours had gone by and it had been dark for more than two. Nak was reasonably sure the police in the second-class car would now be asleep, but the only way to know for sure was to go and see.

Lup Law became aware of the bumping of the train and the wind blowing in his face from the open half of the window. The purser had been through earlier to turn out the lights. Lup Law had slipped him twenty *baht* to ensure he was awakened before the train arrived at Hua Hin. Now everyone in the car was sleeping, stretched out as flat as possible in the reclining seats. A few snored quietly.

Lup Law raised his arm slowly and looked at his watch. It was past 9:30. The purser would be by shortly to wake him. He closed his eyes and allowed himself to drift off.

Most of the people in the third-class cars were now asleep. A few of them watched out the windows and there were one or two quiet conversations. A teenage couple, still with their school haircuts, were quietly pawing each other in a corner.

"*Pay Nay, Khrap*?"

Nak turned and looked at the purser who was standing by the door of the car. "I'm looking for my cousin," Nak said.

"Your cousin?"

"He was supposed to have gotten on at the main

terminal in Bangkok. I got on at Samsen. We were to meet on the train."

"That was over three hours ago," The purser said. "You're just looking for him now?"

Nak grinned. "You don't know my cousin. If you did, you certainly wouldn't want to spend three hours chatting with him on a train. It's bad enough I have to spend the weekend with him in Hua Hin."

The purser studied him, then smiled, and shook his head. "Well, you've only got one more third-class car in front of you. After that, it's second and first class. Might he be in second?"

"Could be. He's got enough money. Could even go first class if he wanted to, but he doesn't like air conditioning. Maybe I'll get lucky and he won't be on the train at all."

"Well, good luck, then," the purser said and gestured for Nak to continue.

Nak walked to the end of the car and then glanced back over his shoulder, but the purser went through the opposite doors of the car without looking back.

Sam and his partner had been called to break up a teen party in a local park. The kids weren't cooperative, so they had to call for reinforcements. When the extra officers arrived, they began loading the kids into the back of the wagon when one of them suddenly lashed out at Sam. When he arrived home the next morning, Sam had a pretty good shiner. A wide-eyed two-year-old Jeff reached out and touched his father's eye, causing Sam to wince. Jeff then burst into tears.

Just as Nak expected, there were no cops in the first of

the second-class cars. It was nearly empty, just a few sleeping Chinese businessmen and a tourist couple who either didn't want or couldn't afford the air-conditioned comfort of first class. The couple was awake but barely noticed Nak as he strode purposefully through the car.

Nak stopped and took a few deep breaths in the passageway between the second-class cars. His heart was acting as though he had just run several kilometers and he could feel the sweat beading on his forehead. He stepped up to the small window in the door to the next car.

Six uniformed cops were grouped together near the centre of the car. They all appeared to be sleeping, but four of the six were in window seats. This would make it more difficult to get at their weapons. Of the two remaining cops, one had no visible weapon and the other had his gun strapped to his leg. The leg itself extended into the aisle, which made it easy to get at, but the weapon was held in its holster by two leather safety straps. These had snaps that would have to be undone before Nak could remove the gun. It was a stupid design, Nak thought. It meant that the officer had to deal with two straps every time he needed access to his weapon. That could only slow the cop's reaction time.

There was only one other person in the car, but this person was in the window seat immediately to the right of the door and so Nak could only see a leg with a hand lying limply across it. The pants were a civilian cut and the limp hand indicated that this man was also asleep.

Nak opened the door to the car and entered. The soft creak of the door and the sound of his own breathing were amplified. He kept his focus on the group of sleeping police officers in front of him. None of them stirred. He slowly walked down the aisle and lowered himself onto the floor beside the cop whose gun he wanted. He reached for the holster.

Lup Law had been dreaming but, though his eyes were still closed, he was now thinking about Chiang. What was she doing now? Though he had been angry, now there was regret. Would he ever see her again?

There was a loud snort and one of the cops in a window seat shifted his position. Nak stopped in mid-reach and waited for the color to return to his face. His hand found the first of the snaps and lightly touched it. To his surprise, it popped open. The cop's head moved slightly. Nak waited an eternity with his hand poised over the second snap. Then he reached for it and touched it in exactly the same manner that he had touched the first. This time nothing happened.

Chiang walked out of the hotel with her bag and about 1500 *baht*, enough to live on for a week if she was careful. She had thought about going to the bar across the street and perhaps offering her services to the pimps who worked there. But then she remembered that such an arrangement would mean continuous exposure to men like the Dutchman. In a day or two, she decided, she would call home when she knew only Lek would be there. Her sister would tell her whether it was possible to return.

Nak slowly slipped his thumb beneath the leather lip of the strap and began peeling it toward the snap. There was audible "pop" that made Nak jump, but the officer did not stir. Nak waited a moment and then used his left hand to move the two straps away from the gun. Then he grasped the gun's handle with his right hand and began to extract it from the holster.

Lup Law's eyes opened slowly. A few seats ahead of him and opposite, a man was crouching in the aisle beside the sprawled sleeping police officer. In the dim light, it looked as though the man was adjusting the officer's holster.

Lup Law's own gun was in the bag at his feet. He looked down and noticed he'd left it open. The barrel of the weapon was clearly visible within. He slowly reached down and pulled out the weapon.

"Hold it," he yelled as he leveled the gun at the man in the aisle.

The man dropped, rolled, and came up firing. Lup Law's head jerked through the open window. His gun slowly slid from his hand, dropping onto the vinyl seat, and bouncing onto the floor.

CHAPTER EIGHTEEN

Sam's eyes flew open and he looked around him only to see confusion mirrored in the eyes of his fellow passengers. There was a commotion in the car behind them, that was clear, but it was difficult to see much through the small passageway that separated the two cars. Sam stood up and began moving toward this when the train suddenly lurched, throwing him forward into the passageway.

"They've pulled the emergency brake," said an Australian accent behind him.

Sam picked himself up off the floor and wiped his chin with the back of his hand. It was bleeding. He saw Larry groping on his hands and knees beside his chair and went to him.

"Are you all right, Larry?"

"Yes, I think so. What happened?"

"Someone's pulled the brake. There's something going on in the next car. I thought I heard shots but I don't suppose that's very likely. Here, let me give you a hand." He helped Larry back into his seat.

"Is there a doctor in this car?"

Sam looked up to see a rather frantic-looking purser. His fellow passengers merely looked at each other. The purser said something in Thai, which Sam assumed was the same question. Again, no one responded.

"I know emergency first aid, if that's any help," Sam said.

The man looked at Sam uncertainly for a moment

and then gestured for him to follow.

"I'm just going to the next car to see if I can help," Sam said to Larry. Larry said nothing, but his fingers began playing.

The purser led Sam to the scene. Three police officers were standing around with their guns drawn. These were trained on a young man lying in the aisle with his back to one of the seats. His face was white and he was bleeding from wounds in his abdomen and chest.

Two other officers were pulling the body of an overweight middle-aged man away from a window. This person had obviously been shot in the head from close range. The impact of the bullet had enough force to push his head through the window. Curiously, there was little blood. The face looked vaguely familiar.

"*Sia leow*," said one of the men.

"He's dead," the purser translated.

Sam nodded and then knelt on the floor beside the young man. The man's eyes moved slowly up to meet Sam's. There was a look of recognition and then the man smiled. "*Sa wat dee kap*," he said in a rasp and then slumped forward. Sam cradled the man's head and then slowly lowered it to the floor. He felt the neck for a pulse and found none.

"What did he say?" Sam asked the purser.

"He said hello."

Sam shook his head. "If I were a doctor and this train a hospital, we might be able to do something. But I'm not and this isn't." He stood up. "What happened here?"

The purser looked nervously around the car. He pointed to the body of the young man. "This man was trying to steal a gun from a sleeping policeman. We think the other one saw him and tried to stop him. This one shot him and then was, in turn, shot by one of the officers."

Sam looked at the face of the young man, at the police officer who still held his gun, and then at face of the older man. It was then that he saw the amulet.

* * *

"You're sure you heard them say that there were three officers going to Hua Hin?" Sam asked grinding out a cigarette in the ashtray beside his hotel bed.

Larry was lying on the top of his bed and looking as though he would fall asleep any minute. He sighed. "That what I heard, yes. Three officers were going. The others were joking because they said it was a holiday and not work. And one said that if it was a holiday, Lup Law would be going himself."

Sam pursed his lips. "Apparently, he was going."

"But not with his men?" Larry asked.

"None of the other police officers seemed to know who he was, and he wasn't in uniform."

"And you're sure it was the captain?"

"He has a couple of very distinctive scars on his face and he wears an amulet. It was him."

"And the other man, you're sure it wasn't the one in the picture?"

"Not even close."

"Then I think it was just one of those things," Larry said.

"You mean it's just some guy trying to steal a gun who just happens to have a shootout with a police captain, a police captain who is dressed in civilian clothes and just happens to be in the process of investigating a murder?

And the father of the murder victim, himself a cop, just happens by chance to be on the same train and is unaware, until the shooting actually occurs, that the police captain is there, the very police captain he interviewed earlier?"

"Kind of makes you want to believe in God, doesn't it?" Larry said sounding hopeful.

"Sure, if your idea of God is a second-rate novelist."

"In this country killing a police captain is not a bright thing to do to."

"When you've been a cop as long as I have, you know that there's nothing particularly bright about the average criminal."

"And it is not very bright to try and steal a policeman's gun right off his person."

Sam put out his cigarette. "Yeah, that's the part that doesn't fit. Maybe you're right. Maybe this is just some kind of random thing."

"So what will we do?"

"Well," Sam said after a pause, "two things I know. One is that we were on the right track by coming out here. Even the police captain was on his way here, a long way out of his jurisdiction. That probably means he was expecting to find some answers. The other thing is that the man who shot the captain definitely wasn't the man in our picture. That may mean that the man in the picture is here. And we are here so we might as well take a look around."

* * *

"You're making sure I don't step on a jellyfish, right?"

Sam looked down at Larry's feet in the sand and then

back a couple of footprints. "That was seaweed, not a jellyfish."

"Stuart told me that he once got a nasty burn by stepping on a jellyfish that had been washed up on a beach."

"You stepped on a little patch of seaweed," Sam said, looking at Larry. His friend wasn't enjoying this little walk on the beach. His steps were even more tentative than usual.

"Why aren't there any Thais on the beach?" Sam asked.

"They don't want to be brown. They want to be white."

Sam shook his head. "Is that what it is?"

"They swim at dawn and at sunset. The tourists can have the beach during the day."

Sam looked at Larry again and wondered if this might be the problem. Was he worried about his skin becoming a deeper shade of brown? It didn't seem likely. "Do you want to describe that house again?"

"She said it was a Thai wooden house on stilts, that it was green, and a bit run down. There are a couple of hammocks hanging from trees in the yard and a couple of motorcycles usually parked beneath the house."

"I think we've found it then," Sam said, looking off into the trees. His hand was resting on his hip right where his gun would have been.

"It looks like what she described?"

"Yeah, it does." Sam studied the house. "Ready to sprint?"

"I don't like this," Larry said.

"Next time we'll come in by the road."

"I don't like running."

"It's either that or burn your feet."

"How far?"

From where they stood, on the wet sand next to the water, to the house was about eighty meters. Thirty of these would be across hot white sand.

"You're looking at about fifty paces, give or take a few."

"What if he shoots at us?"

"I thought you said that no one would feel threatened by a blind man leading an old tourist."

"But, we're here now."

Sam sighed. "You're right. I shouldn't expect you to take this kind of risk. I know where the place is now. I can take you back to the hotel and come back myself."

"But then how will you talk to him?"

"That will be a problem."

"Probably he won't be threatened by a blind man and an old tourist," Larry said.

"Anyone ever tell you that you can be quite annoying?"

Larry grinned. "Could you, perhaps, carry me?"

"You'll make it all right."

Larry sighed. "Okay, but you must watch me very closely."

Sam grabbed Larry's hand firmly and counted off. They sprinted quickly across the sand. On the other side were several trees and patches of sandy grass in the shade. Here they stopped and retrieved their sandals from the pack on Sam's back.

"There, that wasn't so bad, was it?" Sam said.

"I don't like running."

As Larry spoke, Sam looked up and saw that a man with a cigarette was gazing down on them from the door of the house. A quick peek at the photo in his pocket confirmed that this was who they were looking for. Sam felt his face blanch and his fists clenching and unclenching.

"What?" said Larry.

"Shhhh..."

Sam smiled up at the man. It had been absurdly easy. They had shown his picture to a few of the chambermaids at the hotel and one of them had directed them here. They were all giggly and said they thought the man looked like a TV star. Sam didn't know about that, but the man bore a superficial resemblance to Elvis.

"We've found him," Sam said quietly to Larry. "He's looking down on us from the doorway of the house."

Larry swallowed and his hands began playing. "Does he have a gun?"

"He has a cigarette."

"No gun?"

"Not that I can see."

"What do you want me to say?"

Sam looked long and hard at the smoking man. He seemed interested in them but nothing about his manner suggested that he felt threatened by Sam and Larry, or that he would be a threat to them. But this was Thailand, Sam reminded himself, and body language might be different here.

"What do you want me to say?" Larry repeated.

"Ask him if his name is Ute. And if he says yes then tell him we'd like to talk to him."

Larry exchanged a few words with the man and then turned to Sam. "He says that he is Ute and he thinks that you must be Jeff's father. He has invited us into his house."

Ute placed an aluminum bowl full of water and two cups before them and sat cross-legged on a straw mat. He didn't look dangerous, but he did have the kind of strong, sinewy body that Sam knew, from experience, could move quickly. Behind Ute on a mat in the corner, a man was sleeping. The man looked ill.

"Ask him what's the matter with his friend," Sam said.

Ute took a long pull on his cigarette and then got up and walked over to the sleeping man. He looked down on him for a few moments, took another pull on his cigarette, and returned to sit on the mat. He spoke softly to Larry.

Larry turned to Sam. "His friend is very ill and will probably die soon, but we shouldn't worry because it's a disease you can only get through sex."

"AIDS?"

Larry looked uncomfortable. "He didn't say that but I think that's what he means, yes."

"Shouldn't he be in a hospital?"

Ute ground out his cigarette, looked for another, and came up empty. Sam handed him a cigarette. Ute seemed surprised and spoke to Larry.

"He says your son didn't smoke."

"Tell him my son didn't think I should smoke either."

Ute gave a fleeting smile and gestured back to his friend.

"He says that Bom—that's his friend's name—was in the hospital, but when they realized that he had AIDS, they sent him home with medicine to die here. The doctor and the nurses know that AIDS can only be contracted through sex, but they're still afraid."

"Ask him if he's afraid."

Larry looked uncomfortable.

"What's the matter?"

"That question is too personal."

"Ask it."

Larry reluctantly asked the question.

"He says that he and Bom have had many of the same partners."

"Oh."

Ute began talking and continued to do so for two or three minutes before giving Larry a chance to translate.

"He knows about the death of your son but had nothing to do with it. It's likely he was already in Hua Hin when Jeff was killed, but he isn't sure because he didn't find out about the death until a while after it happened. That's also when he found out they were looking for him. A friend of Bom's who was passing through had seen Ute's picture in a Lopburi paper."

"Didn't the papers down here report the murder?"

"He doesn't read the newspaper much. In any case, for the first while he was in Hua Hin he kept pretty much out of sight. Not intentionally, but because he was working nights."

"The chambermaids knew where he was," Sam said quietly to Larry. He studied the face of the man before him. There was no nervousness there. His delivery was calm, almost matter-of-fact as far as Sam could interpret Thai faces. And there was an absence of smiles. Thai faces smiled a lot. This one did not. There was also something mildly disconcerting about the way Ute was studying him.

"Ask him what work he was doing."

"He was taking care of the girls."

"Girls?"

"The ones who work in the clubs."
"Are we talking about prostitutes here?"
"I think so, yes."
"Then he's a pimp?"
Larry asked the question and Ute shook his head.
"Bom was the pimp. He says he protected both Bom and the girls."
Sam considered this and decided that there was probably some kind of distinction here that didn't exist back home.
"Ask him what he did when he found out they were looking for him."
Larry did this and Ute responded with a one-word answer.
"He says he smiled,"
"Smiled?"
"Yes."
"Why?"
Larry asked the question and again the response was brief.
"Because he was in Hua Hin and no one knew he was coming here."
"So he felt safe?"
"I think so, yes."
"It didn't bother him that they were looking for him because they believed he had murdered someone?"
Larry asked the question.
"He says he just assumed it was some kind of revenge from his father-in-law."
"Revenge?"
This time Ute took much longer to answer the question. Larry interrupted him several times before translating.

"A while ago, when the captain was still a lieutenant, he used to try and take credit for any thing good that happened in the police department. On two occasions he took credit for work that Ute had done. On the last occasion he badly humiliated Ute so Ute took revenge by getting the captain's daughter pregnant and then marrying her. He knew that it would only be a matter of time before the captain found a way to get his own revenge. That was the reason Ute decided to disappear and go to Hua Hin and it was only very good luck that he decided to come here when he did."

Sam shook his head. "Doesn't he realize that by coming here, he made it look like he's running from the crime?"

"He would have had to run in any case. Lup Law is a very powerful man and Ute had caused him a great loss of face."

Sam thought about this. "Why would someone kill my son, in order to get revenge on this fellow?" he asked Larry.

Ute shook his head slowly when Larry asked the question.

"Jeff was killed for other reasons, but his murder gave the captain an opportunity to frame Ute. He thinks Jeff was killed by an assassin probably hired by one of the gem merchants. Your son was a good man who cared about the poor workers in Banmi and he was teaching some of them about justice. Then these people were going back to their employers and asking for changes. Jeff was not popular with the gem merchants."

Sam thought about this for a moment. He spoke to Larry. "If he's telling the truth, then it almost looks like our police captain friend was in on the murder."

"At least he was paid off."

Sam studied Ute. He spoke again to Larry. "But this guy's no angel."

"An angel? No, he is not an angel."

"Ask him if he isn't concerned about the man who recognized him out here," Sam said.

"He says the man was no friend of Lup Law's."

"What about us? Doesn't it bother him that we found him?"

Larry asked the question and the man answered slowly, keeping his eyes firmly on Sam.

"He believes you were sent by God."

"God?"

"That's what he said, yes."

"Ask him what he means."

In response, Ute walked over to a small shelf in the corner of the room and came back with a handful of papers. These he placed on the floor in front of Sam.

"He's just put a bunch of what looks like religious tracts on the floor in front of me," Sam said to Larry.

"Religious tracts?"

"I think so, yes. They're in Thai but they have pictures of the cross and Jesus and all that."

Ute began speaking slowly and with emotion.

"In his life he has done many bad things. He has beaten people, stolen, cheated, and taken bribes. He has used his good looks to have his way with many women. He even used them to seduce the captain's daughter, get her pregnant, and then marry her—all without ever caring about her. It was revenge on Lup Law but it didn't work. He did not feel any better. Ute would get drunk, and beat her. In his life he has done many awful things and he thinks he will die painfully like his friend and come back as a dog."

Ute picked up one of the tracts and pointed to a picture of Christ on the cross.

"Being nailed to a cross must have been a terrible way to die. In Thailand we would say he had very bad karma, that he must have done many bad things. But this paper says that Jesus did not do anything wrong, that he was God and did only good things. It says that when he died on the cross he took all our bad behaviors, that he took all our punishments for us."

Ute put the tract down and looked intently at Sam.

"Ask him if he got the tracts from my son."

Larry asked the question.

"Yes, but he kept them for a long time before reading them."

Ute began speaking softly again and continued to look at Sam as he did so.

"He forgot that he had put the tracts in his bag and discovered them again when he got to Hua Hin. When Bom got sick, he was the only one who could take care of him. Bom had helped him quite a bit when he first got to Hua Hin so he felt obligated. But taking care of Bom and having to stay here most of the time meant that he had a lot of time with nothing to do. That's when he started reading the tracts, over and over again. Gradually he began to understand, but he still has questions. One of the tracts talks about how to pray, so he prayed and asked God to send someone to explain the things he didn't understand. Now, he says, you have come. He believes God helped you find him."

Sam's jaw dropped. "He wants me to explain Christianity to him?"

"Well, to answer his questions, yes."

Sam laughed. "Well, you tell him that you're the answer to his prayers, not me."

Larry seemed uncomfortable with this, but he spoke to Ute. Ute shook his head.

"He says that I am from Thailand, a Buddhist country. He wants you to explain because you are Jeff's father and because you are from a Christian country."

"But I'm not a Christian!"

Again Ute shook his head when Larry spoke to him.

"You are from a Christian country, you will have a deeper understanding. He says because you grew up in a Christian country, you will know about Christian things. Jeff came to Thailand to teach about Jesus so, if you are Jeff's father, you must know about Jesus."

"But—"

"In Thailand," Larry said, "it is said that to be Thai is to be Buddhist. This has to do more with nationalism than religion, but most Thais would be able to tell you the basics of Buddhism whether they believed in it or not. He is assuming the same thing about you and Christianity."

Sam thought about this for a moment. "All right, let him ask his questions. I'll pretend to answer and you can give him the real answer when you pretend to translate. He'll never know the difference."

"That would be a lie."

"A lie?"

"A deception. The answer would not be coming from you. It would be coming from me."

"So?"

"I won't do that."

"Oh, come on...Look, who knows? Maybe this will even further the cause of your faith."

“Jesus told us not to sin. He would not want us to sin even to gain a convert. Such a convert would be suspect, anyway.”

“You're willing to let this man slip away on a matter of principle?”

Larry said nothing, but appeared resolute.

Sam studied the expectation on Ute's face. “All right, have it your way,” he said to Larry. “Tell him I will try to answer his questions.”

* * *

The last pair of socks Sam tucked easily into one of his shoes and then pushed the top of the suitcase down until he heard a satisfying click. Jeff's black Thai Bible sat on the desk where Sam planned to leave it. Of what use would such an item be to him back in Canada? He sat down on the bed with a sigh and caught, out of the corner of his eye, the head of a *cheechak* sticking out from under the largest of the room's three landscape prints. The little lizard was trying in vain to swallow an insect whole, a large one whose wings seemed permanently lodged in the corners of the *cheechak's* mouth. Sam watched him for a moment, willing him to succeed, but the *cheechak* merely shook its head to no effect.

Sam looked at his watch, stood up, and lifted the suitcase off the bed. The cab he had insisted on taking to the airport would be there in ten minutes. It was time to say his goodbyes. He looked back at the Thai Bible sitting on the desk, sighed, popped open his suitcase, and threw it in.

Thankfully, there were only five people in the

guesthouse living room, Haddon, Mrs. Cole, Dr. Eaton, Larry, and Cyril Cole, who sat in the corner reading and ignoring everyone. Everyone but Cyril stood when Sam entered the room.

"Well," Dr. Eaton said grasping Sam's hand, "it appears that your time with us is almost over."

"Yes, it is."

"I thought I'd let you know, this morning we got a card from the pastor of the Pentecostal church in Hua Hin saying your friend, Ute, is doing fine."

"Well, I'm glad things are working out."

No one said anything for a moment, but Sam noticed a smile beginning to form on Haddon's face.

"I have to admit, the last thing I expected when you arrived here was that you would wind up doing our work." Haddon shook his head.

Sam looked beyond him to Larry. "How's the Casio?"

"Fine," Larry said with a smile. "I still have to memorize where all the buttons are and what they do."

"I'm sure you'll figure them out." Sam looked out the window into the night air, hoping to see the taxi.

"Did you find what you were looking for?" Mrs. Cole asked.

"I'm not sure what I found," Sam said slowly. Then he saw the lights of the cab turn into the driveway.

CHAPTER NINETEEN

Lena Harwood looked at the black Thai Bible that Sam Watson had placed in her hands and then back at Sam.

"It can have permanent place on your bookshelf," he said. "I doubt very much if anyone will borrow it."

Lena shook her head. "This was Jeff's. I can't accept this."

"Jeff would want you to have it," Sam said. "Besides, I have his English one."

Lena looked long and hard at Sam Watson. "You're not going to tell me what really happened over there are you?"

"What do you mean? I just spent a wonderful supper telling you all about it."

"And leaving out a few choice bits, I'm thinking". She walked over to her bookshelf and placed Jeff's Thai Bible on it. "It'll be here if you need it."

* * *

Wanlop stood proud before his mother in his new schoolboy clothes. Chiang snapped a picture with the disposable camera she'd purchased for the occasion.

"Are you ready?" she asked.

"Go to school! Go to school!" he said and rushed over to take her hand. "Auntie Lek come too?"

"Yes, Auntie Lek will come too."

The three of them walked down the lane toward his first day at pre-school. In the distance, a monk could be seen walking slowly toward them. Wanlop recognized him first.

"*Phra Tanait*!" he yelled out.

Chiang lifted her eyebrows as her brother approached. Normally the monks would be taking their morning meal together at this time of the day. All three of bowed toward the monk as he greeted them. "You're missing breakfast," she said.

"They're saving some for me," he said with a weak smile. "I wouldn't want to miss walking with Wanlop to his first day at school."

Chiang studied the face of her brother. He looked spent. She knew that he found following the 227 precepts required of Buddhist monks to be almost impossible, but his status as one of the Abbott's favorites meant that he had to put in the maximum effort.

"Postman! Postman!" shouted Wanlop.

Everyone turned to see the motorcycle approaching. It was early for mail delivery.

The motorcycle pulled up to them. "I might as well give you this here," the postman said, handing Chiang a large envelope. "Saves me driving to the end of the lane."

"Thank you," Chiang said looking at the letter.

"What is it?" Lek asked.

"It's from Hua Hin," said Chiang.

"Hua Hin?" Lek said. "You don't suppose..."

"Only one way to find out," Chiang said. She tore open the envelope. Several well-worn Christian tracts fell out and landed at her feet. Tanait reached down and picked these up. Chiang was holding a letter in her hand.

Dear Chiang,

I owe you a thousand apologies and can never make right the way that I treated you. However, I have recently come into an unexpected inheritance. My friend, Bom, passed away and left everything to me in his will. I have wired this money, about 100,000 baht, to our account in Banmi. I have no need of it where I am and felt that you could use it to raise our son. I will keep you in my prayers as long as I am able.

Ute

Chiang read the letter aloud to her brother and sister.

"That's amazing!" said Lek.

"It doesn't sound like he's planning to return," Chiang said softly.

"Probably a good thing."

"What are these?" Tanait said, holding up the tracts.

Chiang looked at the tracts in the monk's hands. "They look like the little Jesus books that Jep gave Ute a few months before he was killed."

"You don't suppose..." Lek said.

"Everyone knows that Ute didn't kill Jep," Chiang said firmly.

"Then why..."

"Perhaps this is why he sent you the money," said Tanait holding out the tracts.

"He's become a Christian?" Lek said.

Chiang shrugged. "He's not coming back. That's all that matters."

"And he's sent you a lot of money".

"No amount of money..."

The three adults looked at each other in silence.

"Go to school?" Wanlop asked hopefully.

Chiang looked down at her son. "Yes, and we'd better hurry or we'll be late." They began walking down the road again.

"Do you want these?" Tanait asked his sister, holding out the tracts again.

Chiang thought about Jep and then she thought about the Dutch man. "No."

"Then do you mind..."

"You read them and then tell me what they say," Chiang said.

Tanait stashed the tracts in his robe.

About the Author

G.J.C. McKitrick lives in Sherwood Park, Alberta, with his wife. He has a B.F.A. in Drama from the University of Calgary and a

Master of Christian Studies degree from Regent College in Vancouver. His first novel *A Rose in the Toaster* was written as a partial fulfillment of his master's degree thesis. In the late 1980s he and his family lived for four years in rural Thailand and his second novel *A Walk in the Thai Sun* came out of that experience. These days he writes poetry, songs, short stories, novels, stage plays and essays under the name G.J.C. McKitrick and speculative fiction under the name T.K. Boomer. Although three of his stage plays have been produced, he has not pursued the publication of his fiction until recently. He is currently working on a science fiction epic called *The Fahr Trilogy* and several short stories and songs.

CPSIA information can be obtained at www.ICGtesting.com
Printed in the USA
LVOW11s0123250614

391501LV00003B/23/P